TAMARACK SUMMERS

TAMARACK SUMMERS

Marc Douglass Smith

atmosphere press

PROLOGUE

It was the first hot day in May and old Martin was snoring so loud that it sounded like soft summer thunder. All the birds in the buzzing cherry tree looked like they were ready to scatter before a storm. At least once he murmured the name "Cress" in his sleep. Then he whispered the name again as he shifted in the swaying hammock on the porch of a big yellow house.

Bumble bees hummed and hovered over pink and white blossoms in the garden near the porch. A crow with shiny black feathers toddled back and forth on the newly painted porch floor, and from time to time he cocked his head and peered up at the snoring old man. Then he muttered to himself, started his wobbly walk again, clicked his black bill, and hummed a deep-throated gurgling song only a crow would love.

There came a thumping sound of heavy steps and old Martin woke up with a sudden jolt and almost fell clear out of the hammock. At the same instant, the crow flew off, his wings beating fast. He called out in a very *crowish* voice: "Oh, *go* away, go away, go away...."

"Uncle Marty," as his family called him, looked up and saw that it was Rory coming up the porch steps. Shaking his sleep away, Uncle Marty could smell damp lilacs and roses. The spring sunshine warmed his skin after the chilliness he felt during his dream. He reached for his glasses on a small side-table, put them on, and squinted like a near-sighted possum in Rory's direction.

"Rory! My goodness, what a nice surprise! My great grandnephew has come to see me, and don't you look dapper today?"

Rory, aged seven, wasn't sure what "dapper" meant, but he thought it might have something to do with the clothes he was wearing, so he stopped to take a quick look down at his striped t-shirt, tan shorts, and maroon socks.

"Uncle Marty," he said very seriously, "today's your birthday and Mom wanted to remind you to come to dinner...and she's making a cake!"

"Oh, I see," Uncle Marty said. He rose very slowly from the hammock, swayed a little, and patted down his wispy white hair with two shaky hands. As he looked down at Rory, he noticed how much his nephew looked like him when he was a boy—the same green eyes and splash of summer freckles on his cheeks—but Rory was slightly taller and with darker hair.

"You okay, Uncle Marty? I didn't mean to wake you up. You sounded all sneezy and snorey and kind of.... gassy."

"Gassy? Really? Well, I'm just fine, Rory. Fit as a fiddle." Then he let out a full-body sneeze so loud that all the bees in the blossoms buzzed away.

"Are fiddles fit, Uncle Marty?"

"Just an old saying.... now come into the sunshine

here, Rory, so I can get a good look at you. Hmm. I do be-lieve you're quite a bit taller this year. Yessir, you are."

Rory nodded and smiled. He loved to visit Uncle Marty because he always told the best stories—even if they weren't all true. But now he remembered the reason his mother sent him over.

"Mom said that she can come pick you up at five o'clock because you're kind of forgetful and...." His voice trailed off. Had he said the wrong thing?

"Oh, that's okay, Rory. I guess I might be a little for-getful these days, but I *am* almost...wait a minute now...oh, who cares how old I am? Let's just say there'll be enough candles on my cake to start a bonfire. But anyway, Rory, come on in. I've got some iced tea and maybe I could find some cookies. How about that?"

As they walked past the thick oak door and into the big yellow house, Rory could feel the welcome coolness inside. His eyes grew wide as he was surprised again at the sheer size of the rooms with their high ceilings. He looked at the red-brick fireplace, the wide stairways with the shiny ban-ister, the mantle with a large mirror over it. The grandfa-ther clock in the corner was now taller than Uncle Marty who always looked small as a sparrow inside his own house.

They walked over to a bright corner of the living room that had a raggedy stuffed chair and smelled like pipe to-bacco. Rory knew this must be Uncle Marty's favorite spot because the wall next to the chair was filled with framed family photos and scenes of lakes and woods. He stood in front of the wall and looked at all the photos.

Rory didn't recognize some of the older people in the photos, but they all seemed to be standing in a place where there was thick wild woods and misty water and large rocks of all sizes along shorelines. Some were old black-and-white photos, and to Rory, they looked like they were out of another age where the shadows were deeper, and the sunlight fell in flat white patches on dark waters. Some old photos were in color almost richer than any colors in the world that Rory saw from day to day.

In the center of the photos, there was one face he immediately knew. "There's Aunt Cress," he said pointing to a photo of a young woman with wet hair and green-gold eyes that seemed to look through time and meet his own. "I sure miss her," he added.

"Oh, me too, Rory. It's been two years now since she passed. I miss her every minute of every day." Martin shook his head sadly, his throat tightened, and he let out a long sigh.

At the very top of the wall, above all the other photos, there was a large photo of a turtle. The turtle had a shiny black shell lined at the edge with small red squares. It was sticking its yellow-striped head and neck far out of the shell and seemed to be looking straight into the camera, as if to say, "Well, HELLO there, folks!"

Rory wondered why Uncle Marty had a turtle—of all things—among the family photos, but then he decided that he better not ask. Uncle Marty was about to sit in his favorite chair, the one that looked like it was sinking in the middle and had some white stuffing coming out of it. He turned his back to the chair, started to squat down, winced a bit, and then lost his balance and fell backward. He landed with such a loud thud that it was amazing the whole chair didn't instantly splinter on the spot.

Finally comfortable and settled, he looked toward Rory

who sat on a nearby stool.

"I'll bet you wonder why I have a big photo of a turtle included with the family photos, eh Rory?'

"Well, I really wasn't going to ask you, Uncle Marty, but now that you brought it up...."

"That's okay, Rory. You see, I believe that turtles are wonderful creatures. They might not be as pretty as a deer or a songbird, and they're kind of slow, and sometimes they keep to themselves, *but*... but if you take your time, and you care enough about them, you can be friends with a turtle."

Rory wasn't at all sure about this. "But how can you be friends with a turtle, Uncle Marty? They don't do anything that's fun. You can talk to a dog or a cat or a horse and sometimes they know what you're saying, but you can't talk to a turtle."

"Well, that's not quite true," Uncle Marty said. "What if I told you that a turtle was my dearest friend?"

"*That* turtle?" Rory pointed to the framed photo of the turtle on the wall.

"That's right. Her name was Myra, and I used to see her every summer at our family camp up in the mountains, way up north."

"But did you really talk to the turtle, Uncle Marty?"

"Not only did I talk to her, but she talked back!"

"Really?" Rory had a hard time believing this, but then again Uncle Marty *did* tell good stories even if a few of them were probably not true. "Could you tell me about Myra, Uncle Marty?'

"I sure will, but first let me get some iced tea and cookies and then we'll call your mom to tell her we'll be awhile. So, sit tight, Rory, and I'll tell you about my summers with

Myra. By the end of the story, I promise you'll always love turtles—and maybe otters and snow geese too. You see, they come into the story later on. I guess it's also a story about me too, way back when I was about your age. That's when all the wild creatures were never far away."

Rory nodded his head happily. He was ready for a story. At that same moment, the crow had returned to the front porch and was listening at the open window. He began flying off, flapping his wings furiously as he let out a long series of loud caws—at least it sounded that way to Rory's ears.

To Uncle Marty, the crow's words came through loud and clear: "Oh, come on now," the crow called out, "let's get on with the story! Just let it fly!"

CHAPTER ONE

Martin was just a boy in those days so long ago. He had some magic about him, but only the wild creatures who watched from a distance knew for sure. They could see it in his walk and the way he paused and listened. They saw it in the way his straw-colored hair swirled wildly around his head. To the watching deer, the birds, and the bears around the lake, he was a quick, wild pony of a boy.

"Three Tamaracks" was a slender, wooded point of land that reached out like a long, crooked finger into the cold waters of Orenda Lake. The camp was named after the tamarack pine trees that grew near a cottage. The cottage had bark on the outside logs, a stone chimney that let out smoke day and night, and two covered porches—one down and one up— with a view of the lake.

Surrounding the camp were the very old mountains found in the Adirondacks in the north of New York State. They say that magical things can happen around old mountain ranges, especially for children and the old folks who still had dreams about wild animals and the gnarly faces peering out of the oldest tree trunks.

The three tamarack pine trees, not too far from the large round rocks at the end of the point, were green in the warm months of late spring and summer. Their needles turned gold in the fall when cold winds swept out of the west and moved over the chilly waters of the lake. When the winds were very strong, you could sometimes hear the tamaracks sing as the wind strummed their soft-needled branches. It was a very sweet sound.

Martin was now just going on ten years old. He was adopted when he was seven by two kindly people. They were much older than the parents of his friends back home. His new father's name was Cyrus. When Martin was first adopted, he had a real problem pronouncing Cyrus's name, so he called him "Cider," and eventually "Papa Cider." The name stuck.

Papa Cider was tall, lean, long-limbed, and had wispy silver hair that never wanted to stay in place. He had thick eyebrows and wore rimless glasses. When he smoked his pipe, which was very often, he had a thoughtful, distracted look. He was also always kind to Martin, and if Martin did something wrong, Papa Cider had a way of turning to his wife Nonie. Nonie could be a little sterner with Martin who was a jumpy, energetic boy.

Nonie was a short and sturdy woman in contrast to Cider, who was tall and stringy-thin. She had flushed apple cheeks and always seemed to have a barely contained delight over the fact that Martin had come into their lives. She laughed a lot and wore straw sunbonnets on hot days. She sang to herself, and it seemed that every morning she would come up to Martin, touch his sun-bleached hair, look into his water-green eyes, and say, "What a blessing you are, my boy!" When she said this, sometimes Martin could see tears in her steady dark-blue eyes.

Sometimes when he lay in bed at night in the cabin, Martin could hear the loons on the lake calling to each other in piercing, trilling voices from long distances. He felt lonely then, and he often remembered Father Horrigan's Home for Boys where he'd lived as an orphan. On some nights when he lived there, he could hear owls hooting in the far-off woods in the dark hours. It was a pretty lonely sound.

But Martin knew now that he had found his home when he listened to Nonie and Papa Cider in the other room saying "goodnight" to each other as they prepared for sleep amidst the smells of damp balsam needles and the last smoke from the fireplace.

A favorite time for Martin was at sundown when he would sit on the balcony porch of the cottage and watch the last deep shadow rise higher and higher on Patchen Mountain at the north side of the lake. Pretty soon only the stony top of the mountain caught the sunlight, and it looked like a last hot flame in the dark sky as nightfall arrived.

Martin would usually sit on Papa Cider's knee as they took in the sights of the lake from the second-floor balcony porch. On cloudless nights they could see the stars reflected on the lake's still waters. Fish or snapping turtles would nose up to the surface and circles would form in the water. Occasionally a fish would jump and all the stars in the sky would tremble for a few seconds.

Martin, beginning to feel sleep coming on, would do his best to follow Papa Cider's hand that would sweep across the sky. He'd softly call out the names of constellations—Martin liked the sound of the names, especially "Aquila" and "Ursa." Eventually, he would fall asleep. Papa Cider, looking down at the face of the sleeping boy, would say, "Oh, it might be bedtime for Martin. Yep, even the big bear in the sky is getting sleepy now."

With that, Martin felt himself swept up into Cider's arms, down a stairway, and his weightless dreaming was about to begin as he was lowered onto the bed.

After that, Papa Cider might walk out into the living room and drop a last log on the fire.

Then there was a sudden burst of firelight on the wall of Martin's bedroom, and he'd open his eyes for a second and look at the pine knots in the wall. Each one looked like the dark, alert eyes of a deer, or sometimes a moose, or a bear cub, or other creature that he might have seen in the woods that day. When the firelight grew low, Martin could no longer see the knotty eyes, but he believed they were still watching over him in the dark.

CHAPTER TWO

There was a small cove on the west side of the camp. It had a sandy beach curved like a horseshoe which enclosed a small lagoon of shallow water. A large round rock jutted out of the water about twenty yards out. This marked where the water became deep and Martin had strict instructions to never swim past the rock if he were alone.

The cove was Martin's favorite place to be during the summer days. He'd wade in the shallows and watch small fish gather around his toes. Sometimes small trout or perch would visit the waters of the cove, but they wouldn't stay long. The sand on the beach was clean and white. Martin would bring to the beach a duffle bag that was filled with plastic toy soldiers. He'd open the bag, spill the soldiers out onto the beach and then begin to place them in one of the several sandcastles he'd made. They were weathered, tired old soldiers who looked like they'd been through a few wars and might be too weary and worn thin to want to play.

One morning, only a few days into the summer vacation, Papa Cider and Nonie were reading the morning papers on the long, covered porch in the front of the cabin. Both would glance up from time to time to see what Martin was doing down at the beach. Papa Cider set down his newspaper and looked out to where Martin sat alone on the beach in an Adirondack chair.

"Looks like the loneliest kid in the world today," Cider said.

"Did you ever notice how he looks at his left hand when he's alone, Cyrus?" Nonie said.

"Yep," Papa Cider said, shaking his head sadly. "They didn't say a thing about the scars on his hand and forearm when we adopted him. Just said it happened before he came to the Boys' Home. Got that really big scar on his chest too."

"Oh," Nonie said, "I can't even think about harm coming to that sweet-hearted boy."

"Like I said, looks like the loneliest kid in the world."

"Shush," Nonie said putting her finger to her lips. "Go out there, Cyrus. Maybe Martin needs someone to talk to right now. Sometimes we're so used to being with each other that we forget that he's just a little boy who wants someone to talk to."

Papa Cider mumbled to himself, "Well, he does such a good job of entertaining himself, but then again...."

With that Cider was up from his chair and heading down the path toward the beach.

As Cider came out onto the beach, he noticed one particularly fine sandcastle that Martin had built. It was really more of a fort with the tired blue and gray Civil War soldiers on watch.

"That's one fine fort you built there, Martin," Cider said as he approached.

Martin shrugged. "The wind will take it away. There's always wind on this lake."

Cider reached down and, with surprising strength, easily lifted Martin onto the green Adirondack chair at the back edge of the beach and set him on his feet and looked him straight in the eyes.

"What's wrong, Martin? You seem sad lately."

"Nothing, Papa Cider. I'm fine."

"Oh, come on now," Papa Cider said softly, "you don't look fine to me."

Martin took a deep breath and then said it, a little painfully, "There aren't any children here."

"I know," Papa Cider said. He now sounded sad himself. "Just the three of us here."

"Don't get me wrong," Martin now said with a little alarm in his voice, "because you and Nonie mean...well you're *everything*... it's just...well...it gets a little lonely sometimes."

Papa Cider looked at the sky for a second and then looked back at Martin: "Do you remember those slinky, slippery otters we watched playing on the dock this morning?"

"Sure, Papa Cider. They were having fun."

"Hear those loons calling back and forth all day and night?"

"Yep."

"And those crows yapping away up in that cottonwood tree, right now?"

"I hear it all...and sometimes more," Martin said.

"Well, as I see it, we're never alone in a place like this."

Papa Cider then pointed up at the sky to a group of Canada geese flying across the lake.

"Hear that? They're talking to each other all the time as they fly. That bossy guy in front is saying 'Take a left at that big hemlock up there.' Just listen close enough, Martin, and you'll hear all sorts of things around a lake like this."

Martin's mood was brightening now.

"Tell you what," Papa Cider said cheerfully, "how about if you and Nonie and I take the canoe down to the Big Marsh tomorrow morning? Something amazing always happens down at the Big Marsh. Remember that big black bear that swam right in front of us last year?"

"Oh, yeah," Martin said, now completely excited. "Maybe I'll find a friend down there."

Papa Cider paused, hearing this. A friend? Did Martin mean one of the wild creatures down at the Big Marsh?

"And maybe we could have pancakes for breakfast before we go!" Martin said, now sounding completely delighted.

"Yep," Papa Cider said, "Nonie's buttermilk blueberry pancakes. Those are so good, they're like these little *miracles* rising right in front of your eyes!" Now Papa Cider sounded excited even though it was only pancakes they were talking about.

"Miracles!" Martin repeated happily.

When Cider walked off and headed to the cottage, Martin felt some real excitement. It wasn't just that he loved going down to the Big Marsh. It was also that he had a feeling deep-down that something special was about to happen to him. He couldn't quite explain it, but the feeling was there.

At that very second, a crow landed on a limb of a cottonwood tree near the beach. Martin looked up and saw that the crow was carrying a gold ribbon in his beak. He called out, "Nice ribbon there, Crowy!" The crow, seeming about to answer, opened his beak and the gold ribbon blew away.

"Aw, jeez!" the crow said in a sad, squawky voice.

"What did you say?" Martin hadn't expected to hear words from a crow.

"Nothing," the crow said.

"Hey, you said something. I heard it."

"Nope," the crow answered.

"There you go again," Martin continued, "and I'm sorry you lost your ribbon."

"Your fault," the crow said.

"My fault? How so?"

"Well, you called out, and I just had to hold up my side of the conversation."

Martin put his fingers in each ear as if he were clearing them out: "I can't believe that I'm hearing all of this. I guess crows really do talk."

With that, the crow opened his beak, let out a burp, and continued to talk. "I ate two mice, a centipede, and a vole today and, man, it's all starting to back up on me now! I've been having mouse burps all morning, you know those really sour ones. Wait a minute! Hold everything! Up it comes...watch out below!"

Martin covered his head. "No, don't get sick! Not now! Not here!"

The crow let out a cawing laugh: "Oh, just kidding, kid. Nothing on the way up right now. Maybe later I'll have my little afternoon up-chuck."

With that the crow flew off, his wings beating until he was over the surface of the lake. He let out a series of caws that sounded to Martin like "Bye-bye...bye-bye...bye-bye...."

Martin sat there for a good fifteen minutes thinking about what had just happened. Papa Cider was right. All he had to do was watch and listen closely and pretty soon a whole new world of sights and sounds was opening up around Orenda Lake. After all, he'd just had a conversation with a chatty crow who talked about "mouse burps."

CHAPTER THREE

Martin lay in bed the next morning. At first, he smelled the usual fresh cool scent coming off the lake and the dampness lifting from tall grasses and pine needles. Next, he smelled the grease on the hot iron pan in the kitchen—that meant pancakes. These were not just any pancakes, but Nonie's special blueberry pancakes made with buttermilk.

Martin then remembered it was the day to go to the Big Marsh, so he scrambled to get on his clothes. He was just tall and scrawny enough that he could always use a fattening breakfast.

When he came into the kitchen there was a stack of golden steaming pancakes in the center of the table. Papa Cider was already sitting at the table and wearing the baseball cap he used whenever they paddled down to the Big Marsh. Nonie's straw sunbonnet sat on the shelf as she wrapped cream cheese-and-olive sandwiches in wax paper.

Papa Cider rubbed his hands in pleasure: "Well, Martin, it's a fine day for the Big Marsh, isn't it?"

"Yessir, Papa Cider," Martin said as he sat himself in front of the pancakes that were thick with the big blueberries Nonie had gathered from the bushes outside of the cottage.

Nonie bent over and kissed Martin on the head: "Better get to those pancakes soon or your father will snatch every last one. He talked about pancakes in his sleep last night."

Nonie dropped three pancakes onto Martin's plate which he quickly covered with hot syrup that streamed like lava. He dug his fork into the stack, crammed a large amount into his mouth, and, as he chewed, he nodded his head in appreciation to Nonie.

Nonie seated herself and when Martin had swallowed a few more mouthfuls of pancakes, he took a big swallow of milk and looked intently at his two parents.

"I've got this feeling," he said. Nonie and Papa Cider paused in their eating and waited because they knew the clear intensity of that look Martin had when he was excited about something. His green eyes would grow wide and focused.

"I've just got the feeling," Martin continued, "that something special is going to happen today. It's been building up in me all night. It's like something is waiting for me, something really wonderful. Did you ever have that feeling?"

"Yes," Nonie said as she took off her reading glasses and wiped away a tear. "It was the morning we picked you up in the car and brought you...." She couldn't finish the sentence.

"Well, well," Papa Cider said as he set down his cup of coffee, "our Nonie is already choked up about something, and it's only seven-thirty in the morning. Might be a weepy day."

"Oh quiet, Cyrus," she said, taking a playful swat at him.

Martin meanwhile helped himself to some more pancakes.

"Blueberry pancakes from Nonie," Papa Cider exclaimed loudly. "It's just one of those sweet little miracles in life, eh Martin?"

Martin, his mouth full, could only nod in agreement.

"Well, eat hardy," Nonie said, "because it's a long paddle down to the Big Marsh."

Now that he'd swallowed the last of the pancakes, Martin had three words to say: "A little miracle." He said it in a fair imitation of Papa Cider's deep, cranky voice. The three of them laughed. After all, "miracle" is really a pretty funny word when you're just talking about pancakes.

CHAPTER FOUR

Papa Cider and Nonie paddled, and Martin sat on a cushion in the center of the canoe. A wind out of the west was at their backs so the paddling was fairly easy.

They reached the northeast corner of the lake where there was a narrow channel of water that had two towering red pines on either side marking the entrance to the Big Marsh. As they paddled into the marsh, they could smell a sweet scent. The marsh was filled with fields of water lilies and pads, and there was a narrow, clear channel of water in the middle that they followed. Nonie looked out toward the thick lily pads and said, "It looks like you could walk to the shore from here and just pick lilies on your way!"

The current was slow in the channel, so they paddled slowly and easily. There were narrower channels that branched off the side and wended through rushes, brambles, and tall grasses. The water had a coppery tint to it.

They were all quiet as they took in the sights. There were tall, dead, bare trees in the shallows that rose like the masts of tall ships. Some had large, thatched bird nests at the very top. Sometimes a blue heron flew overhead, its wings beating slowly as if it were in no particular hurry to get anywhere.

Something about being in the marsh always moved Papa Cider. He lifted his paddle out of the water for a second, dropped his head back, closed his eyes, and let the sun warm his face. He looked around at the marsh and made a sweeping motion with his hand as if to take in the whole marsh as he spoke.

"This is the inlet. It's where the whole lake begins. Can't even see the current here. It's like the whole lake is born here where the water looks so still."

"Well, aren't you just full of poetry today?" Nonie said, but Papa Cider wasn't finished.

"Just look at all these side-channels...like long arms reaching out as if the lake was exploring and finding its way."

Martin pointed to one of the wider side-channels: "Look. The water level is different up that way. I bet there's a beaver dam."

"Well, let's give it a try," Nonie said, her eyes hidden by sunglasses and the drooping brim of her floppy sunbonnet. "Let's see what those little fellows have built down there."

As they made their way down the narrow channel, a beaver suddenly surfaced and swam in front of the canoe.

"Look," Martin said, "he's leading us to his home!"

"I don't think so," Papa Cider said. "Just watch what he does next."

Almost on cue the beaver slapped his broad tail on the surface and then dived under the water.

"That's a warning," Nonie added. "It means he wants

us out of here. Let's take a quick look and then leave the beaver family in peace."

With that, they rounded the bend of the channel and were soon in front of a beaver dam about five feet high. Behind it, the water was collecting into a large, spreading pond.

Just before turning the canoe around, Papa Cider took a long look at the beaver dam: "Well, will you look at that? I'm an engineer, and I couldn't make a dam that snug if I wanted to. I tip my hat to those chubby, toothy little fellas. There's something awfully smart about them."

They turned the canoe and were heading back to the main channel again. Once there, they let the canoe rest in the shallows close to the shore, and Nonie brought out a jug of lemonade and her very good cream-cheese-and-olive sandwiches made with thick pumpernickel bread. After eating silently and happily, they paddled off again until they reached the channel leading out of the Big Marsh.

"Amazing how fast the time goes down here," Nonie said, her paddle moving smoothly as she sat in the front of the canoe.

"That beaver dam was worth the trip," Papa Cider added.

Martin was quiet now. Where was the wonderful thing that he just *knew* was going to happen on this day? But no sooner had he said that when they passed a big red smooth rock near the shore. At first glance, it looked like it had a small, smooth dark stone on top of it. But as the canoe passed within ten feet, a long neck and head poked out of the "rock"—it was a turtle, a small baby turtle. Martin knew his turtles, and this was a baby Painted Turtle with yellow and red stripes on its neck, legs, and tail.

"Look!" Martin cried out, "That baby turtle is all alone out here. Wow, she's so tiny!"

Although the canoe was not that far away from the rock, Papa Cider let his paddle rest on his lap, took out his binoculars, and focused on the small turtle.

"I'm not sure how you know it's a 'she,' Martin, but it's a cute turtle. Looks like it's smiling. Looks a little like your Aunt Myra, Nonie." Papa Cider knew he might have said something wrong the minute it came out of his mouth.

"Give me those binoculars!" Nonie said a little tartly. She then took a look at the small turtle and then turned her head to address Papa Cider who was already wincing a little knowing he'd said something that didn't sit right with Nonie.

"Cyrus, would you like to explain to me exactly *why* this turtle resembles my dear departed Aunt Myra?"

"Oh," Papa Cider said, trying to get his thoughts together, "it's just the little smile that tiny turtle has... sort of like when sweet Aunt Myra took her teeth out when she just wanted to take a doze in her big rocker."

"WHAT?" bellowed Nonie, so loud you could hear it all over the Big Marsh. "Are you telling me that Aunt Myra— God rest her soul—reminds you of a...a serpent-headed reptile?"

"Well, no. I don't say it in a mean way," Cyrus said meekly. "It's just that sweet toothless smile that little turtle has...."

"Stop, Cyrus! Enough about poor Aunt Myra's teeth— or *lack* of teeth," Nonie said firmly. "You just sound a little daffier the more you talk! I think the sun must have gotten to you."

"Well," Papa Cider continued in his defense, "it's just

that to me some people over time begin to look like creatures from nature, but in a charming way. You know what I mean?"

"No, I don't know," Nonie continued, "so please tell us about this *peculiar* theory of yours."

"Well," Papa Cider continued cautiously, "think of Mr. Chesterton down at the pharmacy in town. He's starting to look like a sweet old possum to me. That is if you could picture a possum wearing glasses. And then there's Doc Lancaster with that big double chin—looks like a heron that just swallowed a big fish. And did you ever notice how cousin Bobby handles his food, especially those raw peas he loves? Looks a big plump, happy woodchuck munching away at his clover. It's not a bad thing, Nonie. It's just kind of a sweet, enchanting thing. Maybe you're right. Maybe I *am* getting a little daffy."

"And so, Cyrus," Nonie continued, now taking off her sunglasses and arching her eyebrows as she gradually savored the question she was about to ask, "just what kind of wild creature do *I* resemble?"

Papa Cider did not hesitate: "You, Nonie? Why you're a swan, the most beautiful, graceful swan I've ever seen. A rare swan."

Nonie blushed slightly and reached over and patted Papa Cider's hand indicating that he was out of trouble— at least for now.

Meanwhile, as all of this was happening, the canoe drifted farther away from where the little turtle sat on the rock.

Feeling a little despair at the idea of leaving the baby turtle behind, Martin suddenly cried out, "Stop! We have to go back. She's all alone out here."

"She's right where she's supposed to be," Papa Cider said gently. "Probably hatched just a week or two ago, and she's out on her own now."

"But she's a *baby*," Martin protested, "and she's looking right at me like she needs my help."

"I'm glad you're such a sweet, caring boy," Nonie said gently, "but she's best left right where she is."

With that Papa Cider and Nonie began paddling again. Soon they'd left the Big Marsh and the canoe was moving at an even pace against the west headwind on the waters of the lake. It would be good to get back home to Three Tamaracks and build a fire, but Martin could not forget that little turtle they'd left behind.

CHAPTER FIVE

It was 10:30, a little past Martin's usual summer bedtime. Nonie, looking thoughtful, sat at the edge of his bed.

"Some great day, wasn't it, Martin?"

Martin nodded.

Nonie reached out and lifted Martin's chin and took a long look at him: "Oh, you took a lot of sun on your face today. Do you feel all right?"

Martin didn't really hear the question. He had other things on his mind.

"Nonie, could we go to the Big Marsh again tomorrow?"

"Tomorrow?" Nonie answered, a little surprised. "Martin, that's a long paddle to do two days in a row." She paused and thought for a second. "You're still thinking about that little turtle, aren't you?"

"Yep," Martin said, his head dropping again. "She's all alone out there, and it's dark and cold in the Big Marsh at night."

"Well," Nonie said, "Maybe we'll go down there again

this weekend."

"This *weekend*?"

"Maybe sooner. Now settle back onto your pillow," Nonie said, placing a second pillow under Martin's head, "because I have something to ask you right now."

Nonie slowly reached over and touched Martin's scarred left hand and arm. "These scars, Martin. You never told us where you got them. Want to tell me now? You don't have to. I'm just asking."

Martin was quiet for a few minutes. He pulled the covers up higher around him. Finally, he spoke: "Well, I was a really little kid, Nonie, so I don't remember much. Just that I...well, I was running and it was dark all around me, but I couldn't see much and then...."

"Then what, Martin?" Nonie squeezed his hand gently.

"And then something lifted me way off the ground...and I turned around to see what it was and you wouldn't believe it, Nonie, but, but it was.... you wouldn't believe it, but...."

"Go on, Martin."

"It was a giant dark bird, taller, why taller even than Papa Cider. It was almost all black with real big wings. It had a big crest on its head."

Nonie steadied herself. "And did the bird give you these scars?"

"Oh, no, Nonie. I was running, trying to get somewhere in a hurry, but the big dark bird was trying to save me from something. It folded its wings around me and the next thing I knew the bird carried me away."

"It was trying to *save* you? From what, Martin?"

"I can't...I can't remember." A tear rolled down his cheek and he quickly wiped it away.

"Nonie, could we talk about something else?"

Nonie moved closer and put her arms around Martin. "Of course, we can talk about something else. I won't ever ask you about the scars again. I promise. Okay?"

"It's just that I get scared, Nonie...scared I might be left alone."

"Oh, no, Martin we're here to stay—but what do you do when you get scared?"

"Well, I guess I turn to the wild animals. Like Papa told me, you just have to look and listen to what's up here in the mountains. Even in my dreams the deer and bears and littler critters gather around me. It's like they want to protect me. Why would they want to do that?"

"That's easy. It's because you're a lovable, wild little boy. Maybe they can see all that. But right now, let's talk about something you can take into your dreams tonight."

"A story?" Martin asked, lighting up at the idea.

"Sort of a story. Just listen now: there's a place called Glacier Pond. Has Papa Cider told you about it?"

"Only about how dangerous it is getting there. Papa Cider told me *that*."

"Well, let me explain it to you," Nonie said, clearing her voice. "At the far end of the lake there's a creek, but you can't see it because a lot of big willows have branches hanging low over the water there. If you paddle up it, it turns into a creek with rapid waters and lots of twists and turns. That's why Cyrus says it's dangerous."

"Let's give it a try!" Martin said.

Nonie sounded stern: "Now calm down and just listen. That creek begins at Glacier Pond, and they say that on some days you can see the Piebald Deer on the shores of the pond."

Martin looked at Nonie. At night she let her hair down. The dark red in her hair was streaked with silver, but in the amber light cast by the bedside lamp, her hair had a golden tint to it. Her dark-blue eyes looked deeper than ever, and to Martin at this moment, she seemed like a magical sorceress telling him about some amazing secret they would share.

"How do you say it, Nonie, the name of the deer?"

"Pie-bald," she said slowly. "It's the rarest deer in the wild, rarer than a white deer. It's white or very light tan over much of its coat but with dark or white spots, and large swaths of broad stripes in many shades of brown or black. Looks like the stripes were swept across the deer's coat by a big paint brush. The few that have caught sight of the Piebald at Glacier Pond say he is the biggest deer they've ever seen, almost the size of a moose."

"I think I've seen it," Martin said, almost in awe at what he was about to say. "I've seen it in my dreams. Hmm. Yep. Looks like he's painted by a giant brush. I wonder who holds the brush."

Nonie looked not at all surprised at what Martin was saying. She kissed him on the top of the head and then rose up. For a moment in her dark-blue night robe with its silky glimmer shining in the amber light of the room, Martin thought she was about to levitate and turn in the air—but he was sure this was just his imagination.

"So think about the Piebald Deer tonight, Martin." Nonie headed for the doorway and then turned around a last time. "Maybe someday you'll see him up close and that just might be good luck for you. It's good to think of beautiful things when you're ready to sleep."

Martin heard her footsteps go down the stairs. What

other magical things did Nonie know but not speak about? He thought for a second about the Piebald Deer. Then he thought about the enormous bird that one day swept down and lifted him away from danger.

But soon enough he was thinking about less graceful creatures, the ones that move slowly along the earth and carry heavy shells on their backs. They too were beautiful and majestic in their own way. Where was that little turtle, *his* turtle, tonight?

CHAPTER SIX

A busy couple of days followed. Papa Cider, with a little help from Martin, took care of chores around the camp. A rail was replaced on the front porch, a windowsill on the tool shed was scraped and painted. The pebbled paths that led from the porch to the beach were raked. Martin helped as much as he could even if it only meant handing tools to Papa Cider or putting used paint brushes in jars of turpentine.

That afternoon Martin and Nonie did a bracing climb up the path of Patchen Mountain where they ate lunch on the rocky clearing that overlooked blue, sunlit lakes in the distance—Upper Gull, Powder Milk Lake, and Paradox Pond.

After the hike on Patchen Mountain, Martin sat tiredly in the wooden Adirondack chair on the camp beach on the small cove. His eyes began to close as he gazed out at the slightly choppy water on the lake. At one point he fell asleep until he heard a flurry of wings behind him.

Turning his head, he was pretty startled to see that one

of the crows had landed on the back of his chair. He had never seen a crow come so close. He raised his hand as if to shoo the bird away, but before he could do it, the crow opened his beak and clearly spoke a few words: "Soon, soon. Not long now."

The crow flew off just as quickly as he arrived, but Martin called after him: "Soon? Not long for *what*?" But the crow was gone, and Martin found himself alone in the chair again. Moving higher in the sky, the crow called down, "Not-long, not-long...not long now."

"Crazy crow," Martin said to himself, but actually he had a lot of respect for the crows who always occupied some of the highest trees around Orenda Lake and seemed to know everything that was going on around the lake. And now he could hear and understand their words.

Just as Martin was about to get up from his chair and return to the cabin, he saw something rise in the water that was the shape of a small oval and was very dark. It looked like a small, wet rock, but it was moving steadily toward the shore of the beach. Then a stretching little head and long stretching neck poked out of the waters. Martin could see it was a turtle's head and it was smaller than his thumb.

He leaped to his feet and shouted, "What?"

The small turtle reached the shore and, with great effort, pushed sand aside with its thick dark front legs while his back legs worked constantly. As Martin came forward the little turtle stopped and extended its long neck and looked up toward the boy without any sign of fear. Martin noted that the black shell was bright red and orange at the edges. She (he was sure it was a "she") had yellow and red stripes on her neck; on the head, she had bright yellow spots behind each eye.

"Why you're a little Painted Turtle," Martin said, now squatting down, "and a very pretty one at that."

It must have been the shape of the beaked little mouth that made it look like the turtle was merrily smiling up at Martin who stood casting a shadow over her.

Martin reached down and gently picked the turtle up, placed her on his flat hand, and looked at her closely: "Now I'm sure you're the one I saw down at the Big Marsh the other day."

As he said this, he almost lost his breath when he considered the staggering idea that this little turtle might have also recognized *him*. Was it possible? Had this turtle actually been looking for him?

It was then that he noticed a single line running down the length of one side of the shell—it was a crack! "You're hurt," Martin said with a little alarm. He turned his head toward the cabin: "Nonie! Papa Cider! Come here quick, quick!"

He heard Nonie let out a little shriek and heard feet scurrying down the pebble-stone path to the beach. When Nonie saw Martin standing on the beach, she said in a half-scolding voice,

"Good god, child, you gave me a fright! We shouldn't leave you alone so much on this beach."

As for Papa Cider, his eyes immediately went to the small turtle on Martin's palm: "Well, well, what have we here? Oh, looky here." He sounded as excited as a boy of Martin's age.

Martin extended his arm, bringing the turtle closer to Papa Cider: "She's hurt. Look at her."

"Yeah, I can see that," Papa Cider said as he rubbed his

chin and bent down to see the shell up close. "This turtle's been nicked up pretty bad. Could be a raccoon got ahold of her, maybe a big raptor bird."

Papa Cider continued rubbing his chin as he gazed out at the lake. Finally, he nodded his head as if he'd figured something out. "So, here's what we do. Martin, you know that glue I keep on my worktable in the tool shack?"

"Your 'special' glue'?" Martin said.

"That's right, my 'special glue.' Go get it, Martin, and bring along that tiny paintbrush next to it."

Martin handed the turtle first to Nonie, and she took a quick look at it and then gave it to Papa Cider who held the turtle in his hand while Martin ran off to fetch the glue and paint brush.

Nonie looked at Papa Cider: "Well, it appears we'll have a houseguest for a few weeks."

"At least it will be a very quiet house guest," Papa Cider answered. "By the way, do we still have that big aquarium out in the shack?"

"I've been trying to get rid of it for years."

"Well, we better get it out," Papa Cider said chuckling. "Our very determined boy is not about to give up a turtle, especially a wounded turtle, and it's not as if he found the turtle...no, looks like the turtle found Martin, didn't it?"

Martin returned with the jar of glue and the small brush. Papa Cider set the turtle down on the beach. "Now hold her steady with your fingers on the outside of the shell so I can draw my brush along the crack," Papa Cider instructed.

Martin did what he was told, and the turtle did not struggle as he held her in place. Cider dipped the small brush into the glue jar and got just a small amount on the tip of the brush.

He then brushed a fine line of glue along the narrow crack on the shell.

"That should be enough," Papa Cider said after applying the glue. "You don't want it too thick, just enough to mend the crack but still let the shell grow. That glue will dry pretty fast in this wind and sun."

"But we'll have to keep her a few days," Martin said pleadingly, looking at the other two.

"We've already thought of that," Nonie said. "You can keep her in that old aquarium for a while."

"Until she's healed," Papa Cider added. "After that...well, we'll just see."

Martin knelt down and looked at his turtle friend as she sat contentedly in the sand. "I already have a name for her," he said brightly. "Myra. I'm calling her Myra."

"Oh, poor Aunt Myra," Nonie said, her eyes looking to the heavens. "It's official now: she's had a turtle named after her. Oh, dear me."

CHAPTER SEVEN

The lighted aquarium sat on top of a low dresser near Martin's bed. It was a good temporary home for Myra. It had a few flat rocks, water, moss, and even a couple of small ferns that Nonie had carefully planted in a small patch of sandy soil.

During the day Martin watched as Myra clambered up the rocks or swam in the water or took large gulps when she came upon the morsels of turtle food Papa Cider bought down at the pet store in the village.

Martin often found himself talking to Myra, and he didn't feel funny about doing it. He saw how her shell had mended, and he'd say, "You're doing just fine, Myra. You're getting better."

Sometimes Myra's eyes were closed as she sat on one of the flat rocks in the aquarium and Martin would say, "Are you all right, Myra?" As often as not, when he spoke her name, her head lifted and her long neck extended out, and she looked up at Martin with that merry little smile. It almost seemed that she was about to say something to him.

Martin was fairly sure that it was asking too much to hope that a turtle might speak to him, even though he heard crows speak from time to time. Myra was a simple creature and if she never spoke, it was fine with Martin. After all, he had now adopted her as his own, if only for a time, and wanted only to get her well and eventually release her back to the lake.

When he lay in bed at night and thought about releasing her, he knew it was right to let her return home, but the thought of her leaving also saddened him. She was still a baby, and what would she do all alone on the big lake? She *had* been wounded, Martin reasoned with himself, and who knew what dangers were out there on the lake and in the Big Marsh?

On the other hand, she must be a wise creature because she had come to the one place where she could be healed. Martin knew that reptiles like Myra were not known to be very smart, but he also had the idea that every creature seemed to have a special talent that went beyond the kind even the smartest people had. Birds migrated and traveled long distances by using the stars; whales crossed vast oceans while singing to each other. And now there was a turtle in Martin's life who came to be helped, or was it Martin who was being helped by Myra? In a vague way, he knew that they were probably helping each other.

One night Martin took a last look at Myra before he got into bed. He looked down to where she was standing on the rock and noticed that her shell was now completely smooth—Papa Cider's "special glue" had done the trick.

"You're better. Just look at you, Myra! Good as new."

Martin then yawned and stretched his arms. "I'm going to bed now, Myra." He turned out the aquarium light, walked to his bed, and got under the covers. "Good night, Myra."

Almost instantly he heard a tiny but very clear voice say, "Good night, Myra."

"WHAT did you say?" Martin was pretty shocked and wanted to make sure that he wasn't dreaming.

Once again the little voice said, "Goodnight, Myra."

Martin scrambled out of his bed. It made sense to Martin that if Myra were to say anything it would be "goodnight, Myra" because she heard it every night. Martin turned on the light above the aquarium and looked down at Myra who was wide-eyed and awake and looking directly up at him.

"One more time, Myra. What did you say?"

The little beaked mouth opened, and she said it again, "Goodnight, Myra."

"You can talk! Well...I guess I'm not all that surprised by that. It seems like you've been wanting to talk to me from the very start, right?"

Myra hesitated and then opened her little mouth again: "Goodnight, Myra."

"Okay, okay, that's a good start, but we have to get our names right." Martin then pointed his finger at Myra: "You're Myra. That's *your* name." He then pointed to himself: "I'm Martin. MAR-tin. That's *my* name" He then pointed back and forth between himself and Myra: "Martin...Myra...Martin...Myra. Do you understand now?"

Myra looked up at him wide-eyed and silent.

"Well, that's enough for one night. I'm going to bed now, Myra."

Martin turned off the light to the aquarium and got into bed. There was a silence for about five minutes and then that same clear, very tiny voice said, "Goodnight, Martin."

Martin smiled in the dark. "That was just fine, Myra. You're an unusual little turtle, aren't you?"

CHAPTER EIGHT

Myra was mended and looking very happy and healthy after three weeks. You'd never know by looking at her that there was ever a crack in her shell.

Martin was now faced with a problem: should he let her go so that she could again find her wild life in the lake? Or did the fact that she actually *spoke* to him mean that they had a special friendship and were meant to stay together—even if it meant putting Myra back into an aquarium each night?

But it really wasn't a question at all when Martin thought about it. He already knew the right thing to do and that was to give Myra the chance to return to her home in the Big Marsh.

With this in mind, he brought Myra out to the beach the next morning. He was joined by Papa Cider who was curious to see what Myra would decide to do. Papa also knew the boy was giving up a creature very dear to him, so he was determined to be quiet and offer no advice.

As Martin walked toward the water with Myra in his

hands, he spoke to her as Papa Cider looked on from several yards back: "You're a brave turtle," he said, almost choking with deep feeling, "and have a great heart. I know that's what brought you here."

With that, he set the turtle down at the water's edge of the lake where the waves were now gently lapping at the beach.

"Go on, now, Myra," he said, stepping back. Myra took a long look from the water's edge, looked out onto the big lake but pivoted in place, raised her head, and pushed against the sand with her short, clawed legs as she walked directly back toward Martin.

"No, no, Myra. You're all better now, and you have to find your way home."

Myra didn't move. She stood in his shadow with her neck stretched as she looked up at him sweetly, not quite understanding—why should she go?

"That turtle's not ready to go anywhere," Papa Cider offered, as he smiled looking down at Myra. "Maybe she wants you to come into the water with her, come into her world, if you know what I mean. She's been out of the lake for a while. She might not want to go in alone."

"I know *exactly* what you mean, Papa Cider. Could you get my mask and snorkel?"

"Now you're talkin,'" Papa Cider said with the boyish sense of play that Martin so loved in his father. "We'll just get your snorkel, and you can follow her into the world *she* knows. Oh, how I sometimes wish I were your age, Martin!"

Within a few minutes, Papa Cider was back, and Martin was putting on his mask and snorkel. When the mask was in place, Myra took a gander at him and said "Martin?"

Martin looked over at Papa Cider, but it seemed he heard nothing.

Now, with joy in his voice, Martin said to Myra, "Swim? How about a swim, Myra?"

Martin then fitted the mouthpiece of the snorkel into his mouth and walked directly into the water. Myra followed him in.

By this time Nonie had joined Papa Cider on the beach and called out to Martin, "Not too far now."

"Oh, he's a good swimmer by now, Nonie," Papa Cider said softly, "and he'll be fine."

Martin swam slowly toward the deeper water and Myra's little legs paddled quickly as she followed him. He then dived under the water, and Nonie could be heard letting out a gasp. Myra then went under the water too. Martin, with his mask in place, watched her swim underwater. Suddenly free in the deep water, she glided like a bird, almost effortlessly moving through the chilly depths. All the memory of her plodding slowness on land was now giving way to an easy grace in the water.

Martin would surface from time to time to take a deep breath and then dive down again where his underwater dance with Myra would continue.

Eventually, Martin grew tired, so he swam back to the beach. He came out of the water, and an instant later, Myra followed him onto the beach.

"You've got a friend," Nonie, who'd stayed at the beach to watch the spectacle, called out. She then turned back toward the path that led to the cabin.

Papa Cider followed her, mumbling to himself, "A boy

that loves the company of a turtle. A turtle that loves the company of a boy! Well, what do you know about *that*? It's sure something to behold, isn't it, Nonie?"

Martin dried himself with a towel and sat in the green Adirondack chair. Myra settled and sunned herself for a few minutes and then climbed underneath Martin's chair when the sunlight grew too hot for her.

They sat together for about an hour, and from time to time Martin would talk to her: "What a good swim that was, Myra!" or "What will we do tomorrow, Myra?" or "I've been thinking about what I'm going to do when I grow up, Myra." Myra didn't have any answers but always seemed happy just to be around Martin, and he felt the same way.

On this day, after about an hour of sitting with Myra, Martin gazed up at the clouds. There was a wind that day so the clouds changed shape and Martin could see how the different cloud formations looked like big lacy masks with eyes and mouths stretching and changing shape.

Myra came out from under Martin's chair. She extended her long neck and head and began clawing her way across the sandy beach and toward the lake.

"Do you want to swim again, Myra?" Martin asked hopefully, but Myra, who still spoke very little, said nothing as she moved toward the water. Watching her, Martin wondered if this was the end. Maybe finally her need to return home was stronger than her need to stay with him. But he did want what was best for her, so he called out: "Take care then, Myra. Good luck to you!"

Myra entered the water and never looked back. Martin found himself alone again on the beach.

At supper that night Nonie and Papa Cider could see

that Martin was more quiet than usual. His head hung low as he picked at his food and finally just set his fork down, his appetite gone.

Papa Cider finally spoke up: "Listen, Martin, you did a fine thing for that little turtle. She wouldn't have survived without your help, I'll tell you that much."

Martin looked up from his plate: "But she's coming back, you see. She found me once and she'll find me again. She wouldn't just leave like that unless...well, unless she was looking for her home, maybe back in the Big Marsh. That's the way it has to be, I guess. Still, I have a feeling she's coming back to visit again."

"You know what, Martin?" Nonie looked at him intently across the table. "I admire you, yes I do. You have faith and trust, and a love of wild little things some people just overlook. If you say that turtle's coming back, who's to doubt you?"

"Not me," Papa Cider chimed in, "not me."

CHAPTER NINE

Martin took a fresh, warm homemade doughnut to the beach the next morning. He stood on the beach looking out at the water as he bit into the doughnut that was just oily enough to hold the powdered sugar that dusted the outside of it. Immediately an old feeling of loneliness overtook him as he looked out at the wind-ruffled water on the lake and wondered if Myra would ever find her way back.

When he finished his doughnut, he wadded up the napkin and looked around for a place to put it, and finally crammed it into his pocket. As he was looking down, he heard a small but clear little voice: "Goodnight, Martin!"

He looked down and saw that Myra, her black shell still very wet, had made her way up to him and was at his feet. Her yellow-striped neck extended as she looked up at him.

"Myra...oh, Myra! I *thought* you might come back!"

"Back," Myra repeated, "goodnight, Martin."

"Well, it's morning, Myra, so really what you'd say is 'Good morning, Martin.'"

Myra paused a few seconds and then opened her

beaked, lipless little mouth: "Good morning, Martin."

"That's just fine, Myra. You're a quick learner." He looked up at the sunny blue sky and then back to Myra. "It's a beautiful day, Myra, so what shall we do?"

"What *shall*...we do?" Myra repeated and then again, "Good morning, Martin." It was clear that she was very proud of the new words she was mastering.

"I know," Martin said brightly. "We'll build a sandcastle first, and then let's just swim until lunch."

"Swim!" Myra repeated and then she stood by and watched as Martin began looking for the perfect place to build his castle and place his toy soldiers inside the damp sand walls where Myra could walk like a giant tortoise among the stiff little platoon of weathered soldiers.

"Oh, I see it now, Myra—right next to that big piece of driftwood. It will be the best fort I ever built. I'm just so happy you came back!"

"And Myra...she's happy...me, I am," the little turtle added.

While all of this was going on, Nonie and Papa Cider were playing checkers on a small table in the cabin. Checkers was a game Nonie usually won, but neither cared much about the outcome of the game. Papa Cider was pausing so long before a move that Nonie knew there was something else on his mind.

"Well, Cyrus. What is it? Nobody takes fifteen minutes to make a move in a game of checkers."

"Come on, Nonie," he looked up at her as he shook his head. "You can hear him out there talking to that turtle as well as I can. Says something and then he pauses like the turtle's answering him. Isn't he getting a little old for that? Listen to him—just chattering away as if that turtle...."

"Now wait a minute," Nonie said. "First of all, 'that turtle' as you call her, has a name. When a child names a pet, it's a sign that he's taking her into his heart. The other thing is this: just because we can't hear it, doesn't mean that the turtle isn't talking."

"Oh!" Papa Cider said loudly. "Now that's going too far, even for me. You know I love this lake and all the creatures on it, but to say they...well, I believe they talk in their own language, but not in plain English. Please."

"I'm just saying, Cyrus, that maybe as we grow older, we lose the ability to even *imagine* an animal talking to us. The fact that Martin hears Myra talk is a mystery, but it's a lovely mystery, isn't it?"

"I guess," Papa Cider said wearily. "But there's more to it than that. Someday he'll have to say goodbye to Myra. He's given so much of his...you know."

"Love?" Nonie answered. "Even if he loses her one day, he'll never lose that love. That will last him a lifetime. Hey, we're not that young anymore, you and me. An amazing little boy came into our lives when we're almost old enough to be his grandparents. And some day, some day."

"Oh, yes. I've thought of that," Papa Cider said a little sadly.

Nonie continued, "He probably thinks we'll be around forever. But even when that day comes—and I hope it's not soon—we'll have given Martin the best of ourselves, right? And look at the gift he's given us, Cyrus! So, let's not worry that a little boy is friends with a turtle. We wouldn't want him any other way, would we?"

"Nope, we wouldn't. Hmm. I just remembered what the word 'Orenda' means."

"I used to know," Nonie paused to think, "doesn't it

mean...?"

"Magic," Papa Cider said. "It's an old Native American word that means a lot of things, but I think 'magic' is the word that catches it best."

"Well," Nonie said, "if this lake is all about magic, then our boy can talk with a turtle, right?"

They sat for a while thinking about it—magic, lakes, turtles, children.

CHAPTER TEN

Late August finally arrived and Nonie began packing boxes and Papa Cider brought out the plywood boards that would cover the windows when the cabin sat alone. Three Tamaracks camp would be left to make it through the winter without the family that kept on the lights and lit the fires.

The tamarack trees near the cabin were growing paler now, the green needles turning slowly to gold. The maples and other leafy trees were just beginning to show their autumn colors.

Martin, knowing the time had come to say goodbye to Myra, put on a thick wool sweater. The Adirondack chairs had been moved into the boat house, so he sat on a wood stump at the beach's edge where the sand met tangles of bushes. It was windy on the lake but Myra, who left every day in the late afternoon and returned the following morning, arrived at her usual time. She came out of the water and into the stiff wind as she slowly moved through the cold sand to where Martin sat.

"Are you cold, Myra?" Martin, knowing Myra was a cold-blooded reptile, wondered if this day might be too frigid for her, so he lifted her off the sand and placed her on his sweater, and partially wrapped her in the wool.

He began to talk, as much to himself as her: "It's almost fall now and everything is changing."

From where she sat on his lap, the little firm voice replied: "Yes, fall," she said as if fully understanding what lay ahead. Martin had not yet decided what he was going to say when it was time for the two of them to part. "Sometimes we call it 'autumn,' Myra. Isn't that a pretty word?"

They sat there for a long time, happy in each other's company. Martin thought back to that first day when a small, injured turtle came out of the water, the very same turtle he'd seen down at the Big Marsh. He remembered the first words she spoke and the long hours on sunny days that they'd spent together on the beach.

He'd learned something about friendship even though it was with a small creature that most people think very little about. From the beginning, he knew only that she was a small, injured creature in need of healing. He helped her and wanted nothing in return, but in her quiet way, she gave him so much in return.

Now he seldom would feel lonely in the world. Even something as small and humble as a turtle wanted companionship too.

Martin lost track of time and dozed with Myra wrapped in wool on his lap. Then the voice of Nonie called from the cabin: "Get your things together, Martin! We're leaving right after lunch."

"Okay, Nonie" Martin called back, but he immediately felt a deep sadness.

He gently lifted Myra out of his lap and set her down on the sand. He noticed the beautiful pattern of red squares around the edge of her shell. He got down on his knees to speak with her, and she extended her long neck and blinked her eyes slowly the way turtles do.

"Myra," he said, his voice a little shaky "it's time to say goodbye."

"Good...bye," Myra repeated slowly. She may have heard it before, but it still seemed like an unfamiliar word to her.

"Do you know what 'goodbye' means, Myra?"

Myra blinked her eyes again and took a couple of slow steps closer to Martin and then she said three words to him, very slowly: "Don't...know...'goodbye'...."

Martin felt that stab of sadness again in his heart.

"It means I'm going away, Myra. I won't be here to-morrow. Or the next day. You'll have to look after yourself a little bit more. I know you can do it because you know the Big Marsh. I wish you the best of luck."

Myra looked up at Martin's face for a very long time. She then pivoted in the sand and began to very slowly crawl toward the water.

Martin called after her: "I'll be back next year, Myra. Will you come back?"

Myra paused at the water's edge and then turned her head back toward Martin. "Is this...goodbye?" she said.

"Let's just say it's goodbye for now, Myra. It hurts a little, doesn't it?"

Myra then continued straight forward and as she en-tered the water Martin heard her voice, this time sounding a little firmer but not at all glum: "Goodbye, Martin."

She paddled out to the deep water, the late-day sunlight gleaming on her dark, wet shell. Eventually she disappeared from sight.

Martin stood there for a while looking out at the water. He heard two loons call to each other from long distances. A crow watched silently and solemnly from the cottonwood tree overhead.

He was hungry now, so he turned toward the cabin to eat the last quick meal of another year at Three Tamaracks. He'd always remember the time when the little Painted Turtle had come to him for help. He wasn't sure he'd see her again, but that's how it is sometimes. He did know he'd never forget this past summer with Myra.

CHAPTER ELEVEN

Martin loved nothing more than to look at the Christmas tree in the living room, especially when it was blustery and snowy outside.

The tree, a blue spruce with short needles, had fat, old-fashioned lights of green, blue, red, yellow, and white. Many of the ornaments were handmade by Nonie. She made soft little pillow-like ornaments on which she carefully stitched pictures of a loon, pines, screech owls, deer, and otters, all things that reminded the three of their summer home in the Adirondacks Mountains.

On the very top of the tree, there was a soft heart-shaped ornament on which Nonie had sewn a date, followed by the words "Our First Christmas." It was the date of the first Christmas after Nonie and Papa Cider had brought Martin to their home from the boys' orphanage where he'd lived for a few years in his young life.

Martin liked the dark woodwork in the house, the dim, soft lighting, and the faded flowers on the wallpaper.

He loved in the wintertime to stand by the big front windows when the rumbling plows rolled by and shook the window panes on days when there were winter storms, as there was on this day, Christmas Eve.

The only note of sadness he felt as he looked out to the snowy scene was when he thought of Myra. He could picture how it must have looked up at Orenda Lake in December. He knew the big, tall pines—balsams, hemlocks, and white pine—must be creaking and swaying in the sharp, frigid winds coming off the frozen lake. He pictured the Big Marsh with its bare cattails, beaver lodges covered with snow, and ice everywhere. How could Myra survive her first winter?

He knew that turtles had their own way of hibernating, but would Myra know when or how to do that? She was still a baby in his mind and the thought of her trying to survive her first harsh winter was enough to make him wonder if he should have brought her home with him. But as soon as that thought occurred to him, he dismissed it because he knew that the Big Marsh and Orenda Lake were her true home.

He recalled the first day she stepped on shore, the first words she spoke. As he stood there, he closed his eyes and said out loud, "Keep safe, Myra. I'll be back."

At that very instant Papa Cider came through the door stamping snow off his rubber boots, taking off his wool cap and shaking it, and brushing off his coat on the welcome mat. He had snow in his thick eyebrows, and he must have heard what Martin said.

"What's that, Martin? Were you talking to me?"

"No," Martin said, "I was just thinking out loud."

"Oh," Papa Cider said nodding, "I've been known to do

that myself, especially now that I'm getting older."

Martin was looking at a wooden ornament on the tree that Papa Cider must have cut out on his jig saw, and Nonie had painted three tamarack pine trees on it.

"Papa Cider," Martin asked. "Why are the tamaracks so special? Why didn't you call the camp 'Three Pines' or 'Rocky Point' or something like that?"

"Well," Papa Cider said, now rubbing the cold from his hands. "First of all, we have those three tamaracks at the end of the point. Funny how there's three of *us* now too. And the other idea is...well...a little deeper. You see the tamarack goes through its seasons—green in spring and summer, a gold color in the fall, and then it drops all its needles in winter. I guess it reminds us of change. All things change, Martin. But that's even more reason to love what we have right in front of us—the people we love, maybe a little beauty that tries to reach out. It happens really all the time if we care to look."

He stopped for a second, thinking about what he said, and then turned to Martin: "Of course it sometimes takes years to learn all of that, but I think you understand, don't you, Martin?"

"I *think* I know what you're talking about, Papa Cider."

"Yep," Papa Cider answered, "blessings big and small. For instance, what's that sweet smell in the air right now?" He lifted his nose as if sniffing the air like a hungry wood-chuck. "Now what's that *sweet* smell wafting from the kitchen?"

Nonie heard them from inside the kitchen: "Don't you boys come into this kitchen unless you're going to help out."

Papa Cider tapped Martin's shoulder and giggled as he

opened the door to the kitchen. When they went inside, they immediately felt the heat from the stove and the aroma of sweet pies. Nonie opened the door of the oven.

"Cyrus, get those oven mitts and lift out these pies, please, and don't you dare drop one like you did last Christmas."

Papa Cider bent over and looked into the oven and motioned Martin closer.

"You know what those pies are, Martin?"

"Mincemeat! Nonie's mincemeat pies."

"Yep." Papa Cider said. "Just another one of those little miracles."

"Tonight," Nonie said, now looking at Martin, "tonight the lucky people like us get to sit down for a feast just as friends and family have for a long, long time now. But we can't forget those who don't have much. I passed through years like that with my family and so did Cyrus. And you passed through your own hard times, Martin. So, let's be mindful of that as we celebrate the day."

Cider by now was lifting the second pie out of the hot oven. "Miracles for everyone today," he said.

When Martin got into bed that night, he could see the different colors of the Christmas tree lights that now appeared in blurry patches on the stairway wall that led to his room—soft drops of blue, green, red, and orange that made him feel warm inside. Through the curtains of his bedroom, he could see the snow falling softly outside the window. The old steam radiators that warmed his room would hiss, quiver, and belch as hot water moved through the pipes. He felt safe and warm and also felt a little excitement as he thought of what gifts might appear under the tree the next day.

At the same time, Christmas was when he had memories of the boys' home where he spent the early years of his life. He remembered how he and the other boys would put their stockings up on a mantle of a big brick fireplace in the dormitory. Sometimes there were Christmas parties for the little boys where older people brought in presents and then looked from boy to boy. At these times Martin and the other boys knew that part of the reason for the party was to give the childless couples a chance to look at the boys and talk to them to see if there might be one they would want to adopt.

Martin shivered for an instant as he thought back to those days. He held up his scarred hand and arm in the dim light and looked at it and took a deep breath. By now he could hear Nonie and Papa Cider downstairs quietly placing gifts under the tree. He then repeated something he said to himself whenever he thought back to the lonely days of the orphanage: "I'm *not* an orphan anymore." By the time he was reciting this for the third or fourth time, his eyes were closed and he was falling asleep.

There was some magic in this night. As soon as Martin was asleep, he could feel a bright light pressing on his eyelids. When he opened his eyes, he found he was sitting on a large rock in the Big Marsh. It seemed to be the same rock where he had first seen Myra.

"What am I doing here?" Martin asked himself. "I know this is a dream, but I don't want to leave yet. The sun feels so good on my skin."

Martin looked out over the water with all its white-blossomed lily pads. He watched a great blue heron fly overhead and could see a beaver far across the water pushing a white birch branch as he entered a narrow channel. Martin asked the same question again, "What am I doing here?"

"I don't know, Kid. Why are you here?"

"Who said that?" Martin said. The voice had been surprisingly loud.

Martin looked out over marsh water and saw there was an otter only about fifteen feet away from him, if distance could be measured in a dream. He had a brown coat that was shiny in the water and had a long, strong, lithe body and a long tail that propelled him through the water. He swam closer to Martin and then rolled over on his back and Martin could see his short fat paws, and his tiny, very bright eyes.

Martin had not seen an otter this close before: "I know what you are. You're a river otter and you speak pretty good."

The otter yawned as he continued swimming on his back: "Yeah, I talk. As a matter of fact, I'm known to have the largest vocabulary in all the Marsh. Go on, Kid, toss me a word! See if I don't know it."

"Not right now," Martin said, "but I have a question for you."

"Question? I love questions. Never enough questions." The otter was so interested that he was now very near the rock where Martin sat. Up close Martin could see the otter's broad flat head and shapely muzzle and the curiosity in the little brown eyes.

"My question is this: Do you have any friends in the Big Marsh?"

"Sure, I have friends!" the otter snapped back. "Why wouldn't I? Herb the bullfrog and I happen to be very, very close. Poor Herb! Thinks he has a lovely singing voice. Can't say I care for his singing though. Kind of a belching, farting sound, if you know what I mean."

"This must be a dream," Martin said to himself. "Do real otters talk about belching, farting frogs?"

The otter again swam by on his back, "By the way, is that my own breath I smell? I should really stop eating chives with my breakfast. Do you get a little whiff of onion breath when I talk?"

"No," Martin said firmly," but this is a dream after all, and I'm not sure you can smell anything in a dream."

"Hmm. Interesting," the otter said. "Have you any more questions?"

"Just one more: Do you know any turtles in the Big Marsh?"

"Let me see....turtles." The otter stopped in the water and crinkled his eyes as if he were thinking very deeply. "I know Abacus. He's a bad-tempered old snapper who's always counting out loud. For some reason he wants to count his steps everywhere he goes. Goes nuts if you interrupt him."

"I have to go soon," Martin said as he saw the sky darkening which told him he was about to wake up soon in his dark bedroom. "I have one more question: do you know a Painted Turtle named Myra?"

"Myra? Oh, of course. How could I forget Myra? A

pretty Painted Turtle. She's very fond of her name. Not sure where she got it. Yes, Myra, of course. She's a little sweetheart."

"Is she all right?"

"Don't worry, Kid. We all look out for Myra. We think she must be an orphan."

With this, the otter dived under the water and then launched himself up to the top as he swam off and didn't look back. Finally, when he was about forty yards away, he called back to Martin.

"My name's Cheevis, Kid. Come back next summer and we'll have a chat. Did I tell you about my amazing way with words? Oh, I guess I did. Anyway, nice dream, Kid. Glad to be part of it."

Martin sat upright in his bed: "What a dream!" He wondered: could it be true? Did this otter arrive in a dream to tell him Myra was going to be all right? Just the thought of it made him happy. He wanted nothing more than to see Myra again in the coming summer. The fact that he was told by an otter in a dream didn't seem all that unusual to him.

"Why not?" he mumbled to himself as he began to fall asleep again, "why not?"

CHAPTER TWELVE

Martin, Papa Cider, and Nonie arrived in late June in an old wood-sided station wagon. There was plenty of work to do the first few days. The cottage at Three Tamaracks looked sad and blindfolded with the plywood sheets over the windows. Papa Cider took out the screws and removed the plywood and once again sunlight came into the dusty cabin.

The doors were opened, the windows lifted, and everything and everyone breathed in the clear early-summer air. The crows chattered happily in the old cottonwood tree and Martin knew that summer had officially begun.

Martin and Papa Cider carried the plywood sheets and stacked them at the back of the boathouse. Papa Cider turned on the waterline that went into the house and the parched pipes gurgled and sputtered with new life as the lake water flowed into the plumbing.

Nonie was usually in a bad mood on the first few days after they arrived. She took her broom from the room and would stop, mop her brow, and declare, "Such dust! Dust like I've never seen. A whole winter and this place hasn't seen a broom." She then went to the sink and turned on the tap that spit out its first water: "Filthy!" Nonie said. "Cyrus, how would *you* like to scrub this sink? Frankly, I can barely look at it. Well, don't just stand there with your hands in your pocket!"

Papa Cider winked at Martin: "Well, we're warming up now, aren't we?"

Martin went out to his beach cove and began to pick up pieces of driftwood and other objects that littered the sand after the long winter and rainstorms of the cool spring that followed. From time to time, he'd glance out at the still-chilly water and wonder if he might be expecting too much to see Myra come back after she had endured a long winter at the Big Marsh. She would also be a year older now. Maybe she had moved on to other things that might occupy a turtle who was not quite a baby anymore. It was only natural after all, or so Martin told himself.

What had happened the summer before was magical in a way that might never happen again. On some level, Martin understood that these thoughts were what he used to protect himself from disappointment. In fact, in his heart of hearts, there was nothing that would make him happier than seeing Myra once again. But a whole morning and afternoon passed and Martin returned to the cabin, fairly sure that last summer with Myra was a one-time event.

That night after dinner everyone took their regular places around the fire. Nonie often read mystery stories at night, the kind that usually took place in an English village where it was left to an older woman, or possibly the town vicar, to solve the mystery. Papa Cider leafed through a folder of articles from magazines he saved. The articles often had titles like "Raise Your Own Chickens for the Best Eggs," or "Fifty Nifty Uses for Pipe Cleaners," or "Don't Wait on That Hernia!"

Nonie stood up from her chair, put her book aside, and looked over to where Martin sat doing sketches of turtles in pencil.

"You're still thinking about Myra, aren't you, Martin?"

"Yeah, Nonie. I still hope to see her again."

Papa Cider piped in: "Well, as I always said, you did that turtle a great turn, and even if you *never* see her again...."

"Okay, enough, Cyrus! He gets your point." Nonie shot a scolding look at him.

Papa Cider was a little taken aback by Nonie's sharp words, so he shrugged his shoulders, raised his eyebrows a little, and said, "Well, I guess it's time for me to hold my peace. I was just trying to say...."

Martin stood, stretched his arms, and headed up the stairway, his feet landing loudly on every warped step of the old wooden staircase.

"Any plans for tomorrow?" Papa Cider asked.

"I guess I'll head down to the cove early tomorrow."

"Remember," Papa Cider said, "tomorrow for breakfast we're having my special 'Cider's Own Adirondack Flapjacks,' as I might call them when I sell the recipe. Nothing like them, if I do say so myself."

"Don't plan to swim for at least three hours after breakfast, Martin," Nonie added. "You know how big your father's flapjacks are. You know, recovery time and all of that."

"Thanks, Nonie," he called back as he went up the

stairs. "I just plan to sit on the beach in the morning. Nothing special."

"You sleep tight, son," Papa Cider called after him. He then turned to Nonie and said in a quieter voice, "Well, the boy doesn't give up, does he? Kind of a good lesson to us all, isn't it? And who knows? Maybe that turtle hasn't given up either. Come sunrise, in one or two days, maybe she'll set out from the Big Marsh to find him."

Just then the curtains in the cabin suddenly blew and the fire, for a moment, stoked up and crackled.

"Hear that, Cyrus? There's something playful in the air tonight. Something very good may happen tomorrow."

"If you say so, Nonie. I just hear wind blowing the curtains. You take it as a sign of magic and good things on the way. I don't always understand it, but that's why you keep an old fella like me on his toes. As you say, it's all a lovely mystery, isn't it? To tell you the truth, if that turtle shows up again, you can count me as a believer."

CHAPTER THIRTEEN

As promised, they started the day with flapjacks and not just any. They were Papa Cider's slightly heavy and pasty concoction. The flapjacks were like pancakes but much thicker and larger. They were pan-fried in a little oil and were slightly crusty on the outside and dusted with powdered sugar.

They tasted good but were very gooey and Nonie and Martin knew how much pride Papa Cider took in these gigantic pancakes, so they each ate the entire flapjack that sat like an enormous, sprawling sponge in front of them.

By the end of breakfast, Nonie was searching for an antacid, and Papa Cider went back to bed for an early-morning nap ("Didn't sleep too well last night"). Martin left for the beach and, when he got there, let out a loud belch that caused all the crows in the cottonwood tree to cock their heads and look down.

The mist had lifted from the lake and the sun was burning hot and clear in the morning. Martin sat in the Adirondack chair and every once in a while rubbed his stomach. He let out another belch, and he clearly heard one of the crows in the cottonwood tree say, "Enough already," while the other crows let out a cawing laugh, and one said "gas-bag, gas-bag, gas-bag."

"Those crows again!" Martin said out loud. "Always with their weird comments. What do they find so funny? Too smart for their own good."

By now his eyes were on the lake which was uncommonly smooth this morning. The waters became a shimmering blue as he kept his eyes on the surface, always wondering if Myra might show up. He was just about to head back to the cottage when one of the crows landed at his feet, cocked his head, and looked up: "Bigger," he said and then flew off.

"Bigger? What does that mean?" Martin said, shading his eyes and watching the crow fly off as it called down to him with one more word: "Soon."

He waited awhile longer and grew more discouraged. He shook his head at his own foolishness, first at the idea the crow's words meant *anything*, and second at the idea that a turtle would return to the same place for two years just to see him.

"I'm maybe getting too old for this now," Martin said to himself. Maybe too old to believe in talking, friendly creatures, and the idea that a yapping crow could tell him anything useful.

As soon as he said this he felt sad. But at that same moment, he looked out over the waters one last time and saw a small wake in the lake as some creature was crossing the water. Then he spotted something dark and shiny like a smooth black rock rising in the water. But it couldn't be Myra, he thought, because the shell he saw coming toward the shore was too big. Maybe that's why the crow was saying: "bigger!" If this was Myra coming back to him now, she was surely not the baby he'd left behind last year.

Like a small periscope, a turtle's head and neck came out of the water, but the head was larger, the neck longer than he expected. Myra—if it was indeed Myra he was watching—moved more swiftly through the water than before.

In no time the turtle was on the beach and, by the way she fearlessly moved toward Martin, he knew it was her. The red stripes on her neck, and the yellow ones on her head, were even more vivid in color as was the red edging on her large shell. She stopped near his feet and craned her long neck looking upward at him intently.

"Myra!" he said, his voice quivering with excitement, "you've come back!"

"Myra...me!" she said gleefully. Though she was now bigger—almost a year had passed after all—she still had the same very tiny but distinct voice.

"Oh, Myra, look at you! You're so big and grown-up now—and just look at all your pretty colors!"

Myra, still peering up at him, said "Big...big."

It finally occurred to Martin that Myra was referring to *him*.

"Oh, me you mean," Martin said as he looked down at his own longer legs and realized that he too must be looking slightly different to Myra. "I guess we both grew up a little, didn't we, Myra?"

Martin walked over to the green Adirondack chair and Myra clawed through the sand following him. Martin then stopped just before he sat down: "By the way, do you remember my name?"

"Martin!" the little voice said happily.

"That's right, Myra, That's right. Now why don't we just have a nice afternoon together on the beach, just you and me?"

"Just Myra and Martin!" Myra said gleefully and then quietly uttered one more word, "friends."

"Yes, Myra. That's a wonderful word, isn't it? And that's just what we are—friends. Very good friends."

CHAPTER FOURTEEN

By their second day together, it was as if they'd never been apart. Martin would sit in the Adirondack chair on the beach and Myra, still wet from her morning trip from the Big Marsh, would sun herself until she was dry. As always, eventually, she'd find the shadow under the chair when the sun got too hot.

Martin was reading a book he'd brought from home called *Tortoises of the Galapagos Islands*. Since knowing Myra, he'd become very interested in the whole subject of turtles and their habits and the different variety of turtles that lived around the world.

In the days that followed they continued this routine as they both were very contented in one another's company. Every once in a while, Martin would set down his book and say "swim" and Myra, who knew what this meant, immediately headed for the water while Martin picked up his snorkel and water goggles and ran full-speed into the water.

Myra would paddle about on the surface, and when Martin dived down into the deeper water, she'd dive with him. If anything, she was more graceful under the water now that she was bigger. She'd glide like an eagle through the sunlit waters and occasionally she'd do a fancy move where she'd do a complete flip over onto her back, showing the bright yellow of her underside, and then she'd right herself and continue swimming ahead. All the time Martin watched usually just above her on the surface looking down as he breathed through the snorkel.

Finally, they'd return to the shore and the warm sun and sand. Martin felt happily tired after these swims, so he'd dry off with a towel while Myra waited by the chair. There, they'd sit as the afternoon went on and the sun slowly dropped and all the trees around the lake looked like they were painted with reds and golds by the late-afternoon sun.

It wasn't that they just sat quietly all the time. In fact, Martin would find himself talking to Myra, sometimes for an hour at a time. They were fairly one-sided conversations. Martin was beginning to realize that Myra would always be a turtle of few words, even as she was growing and no longer a baby. Still, when Martin spoke, Myra, her eyes closed, seemed to be listening. Every once in a while, Martin would say something that got her attention. He would see her eyelids open, and her head rise and turn toward him as if she understood that he was saying something very important.

He'd tell her almost everything on his mind, including his fondest hopes and dreams and how he felt about Nonie and Papa Cider.

"You know, Myra," he was saying on this day, "I think one day I'll become a scientist, and I want to become the kind of scientist who studies amphibians and reptiles—like you."

Myra's head rose immediately, "Rep-rep-reptiles?"

"Yes, that's how you say it, Myra. Very good."

"But I'm not a...rep-tile," she said emphatically, "I'm a turtle, a very *pretty* turtle."

"Yes, you are, Myra, and someday I'll explain to you about reptiles."

"Turtle!" Myra raised her little voice, "and *friend*," she said firmly, "*your* friend."

"Yes, you are, Myra. You're my turtle friend and some-day when I'm a scientist I want to bring attention to all of you turtles and creatures like you that get overlooked by a lot of people."

"It's very nice to look up in the sky to see birds, or to look at deer or moose or bears. But you know what, Myra? Since I've known you, I've started to think that not enough people look down to see all of you little creatures who move slower and crawl along the earth. Why turtles like you are...."

"Wondrous," Myra said, "we're wondrous."

"Well, what a good word that is, Myra! Did I teach you that?"

In answer, Myra muttered a word that was really a name, but she said it so quietly that Martin, who kept talk-ing, didn't hear. She said very quietly, "Cheevis." That's where she heard the word "wondrous."

Not hearing, Martin continued, "...and if I can become a scientist, I want to help out Papa Cider and Nonie be-cause they saved me, Myra. They took me into their home and loved me when I felt alone and all broken up. I guess love must be pretty powerful, Myra. It's like it heals you, just like your shell was healed. Love is really...."

"Wondrous!" Myra repeated that word, and now Martin stopped talking and took a long look at her.

"There's that word again, Myra. I don't remember ever saying that to you. Where did you hear that word?"

This time Myra answered, and she was loud and clear, "Cheevis."

"Cheevis?" Martin looked puzzled. "I sort of remember that name, but where did I...?"

"Friend," Myra said again firmly.

Martin was suddenly stunned when he realized what she was saying. He readjusted his baseball cap on his head, and then took the cap off and ran his hands through his damp, sun-bleached hair as he thought about this new information.

"Wow," he said now to himself as well as to Myra, "you have other friends, don't you? It makes sense really. You live most of your time in the Big Marsh and of course, you have friends. And one of those friends is—oh, my gosh—an otter named Cheevis! That's right. I had a dream once where I met an otter in the Big Marsh. Is there anyone else besides Cheevis?"

Myra considered the question and then her beaked little mouth opened again: "Flo-relle."

"Florelle? What a pretty name! And what kind of creature is *she*?"

Myra didn't answer but now was heading for the lake to begin another late afternoon trip back to the Big Marsh. She solemnly moved her limbs and plodded through the cooling sand of the beach that seemed to ripple with waves as fast cloud-shadows passed overhead while she headed for the lake.

Martin, still amazed at this new information, called out to her: "Myra, any friend of yours is a friend of mine. Maybe just bring your friends here sometime, okay?"

Just as quickly she was in the water and gone.

Martin put his green cap on again and shook his head, "Wow," he said, "I should have known. Well, that's the way it *should* be," he said to himself even though he was just slightly hurt in knowing that Myra's world now included more than just him.

As he went up the path to the cabin he found himself laughing: "Cheevis and Florelle? Where did they get *those* names?"

CHAPTER FIFTEEN

At the cottage, there was always work to do during the summer months. Papa Cider would put on his old mud-stained work gloves, climb his ten-foot ladder, and clear wet pine needles out of the gutter so that the rainwater would flow cleanly. This was especially important during the big thunderstorms that sometimes moved in stiff gusts across Orenda Lake.

There were also screens that needed mending so that mosquitos couldn't get into the cabin especially at night when they would hover and whine near everyone's ears.

For her part, Nonie never felt that the cottage windows seemed clean enough for her, so she sprayed and rubbed the glass up to three times a week even though Paper Cider said that if they were any clearer the birds would be flying into them, thinking there was no glass in the window at all. Nonie thought that was nonsense because most of the birds that flew near the cottage were very familiar with the place and the other ones might have to learn the hard way.

There was no room for a washing machine or dryer in the cottage, so once a week the family of three would drive down to West Scotus Village to use the coin laundry. Martin looked forward to these visits because it meant going to the West Scotus General Store. The store's proprietor was a man named Maynard T. Thoxley. According to Nonie, he followed in a line of Thoxley men who'd run the store for 120 years.

The store had everything a person could possibly need, and it was the only store of its type in that part of the Adirondacks. It seemed that everyone—vacationers and people who lived in the area year-round and people simply passing through—went there on weekends even though Mr. Thoxley was known to have a short temper. His temper was especially short with children, and especially with boys about Martin's age. The reason for this, it was widely repeated in West Scotus, was that Mr. Thoxley was sure he had a shoplifting problem. He was also sure that it was the little boys who were the thieves taking candy out of the big glass jars in the front of the store.

Papa Cider, Nonie, and Martin came through the door of the West Scotus General Store at about nine in the morning, and it was already filled with customers milling about the store. Martin loved the old-fashioned look of the store that was right out of a storybook with its unvarnished wood floors that sagged a little. Shelf after shelf had goods and knickknacks and wares, anything from fishing gear to a cheese-and-cold-cuts counter, and a clothing section that had hats, wool jackets, and cotton underwear in just about every size.

It wasn't long before Martin stood in front of the long counter with the big glass jars of hard candy. One jar was filled with butterscotch candies, another with peppermint, and another with lemon drops. Still, another had horehound. Horehound was Martin's favorite. Its special taste was because horehound was a plant belonging to the mint family. Martin found this out from reading a book called *A Children's Guide to Plants and Flowers of North America.*

As Martin stood studying the candies in the jars, he was only a few feet away from the cash register where Mr. Thoxley was cashing out the purchases of customers who waited patiently in line. No one knew exactly how old Mr. Thoxley was because he had looked old for quite a long time. He was shiny-bald on top of his head and had thick, gray mutton-chop sideburns that, along with his darting black eyes, made him look like an alert and very concerned squirrel. He wore half-lens, bi-focal glasses that allowed him to look over the top of the frames and keep an eye on what was going on in his store.

He was at the cash register returning change to a man in a rain slicker who was buying fishhooks, a jar of pickle chips, and a half-pound of bacon carefully wrapped in white paper. As Mr. Thoxley handed the man two dimes in change, he began to speak just loud enough for every-one in the store to hear: "These fuzzy-headed little kids that come in here...well, they're stealing me *blind*, I tell you."

Customers in the store were now growing quiet and slowing down in the aisles as Mr. Thoxley continued.

"Soon as I turn my back, they dip their snotty little sleeves into one of my candy jars! Just look at this jar of lemon candy," he said lifting a nearly empty candy jar up high so everyone could see it. Martin could hear the muf-fled laughter from some of the customers who had proba-bly heard this all before.

"Not funny," Mr. Thoxley said, his bushy eyebrows rising above the frames of his glasses, "Not funny at all. This jar has gone down just since this morning, and I haven't sold one bag of candy...so where did it go? I'll tell you where: it went into the linty pockets of those little boys who wander in here like... well, like little raccoon bandits! I hate to say it that way, but that's what happens the minute I leave this counter."

He shook his head one more time as the next customers stepped up to the cash register.

"Maynard T. Thoxley cannot watch *all* the store *all* the time," he continued, "but there's not anything wrong with these eyes." At this point, he took off the glasses and pointed to his eyes for dramatic effect. "Still got twenty-twenty vision, the eyes of an eagle! It's just things up *close* that go a little blurry on me."

Martin looked back to where Nonie was standing a few feet back and saw her roll her eyes and giggle to herself. She stood in front of a revolving rack of paperback books and Martin was sure that Papa Cider must have been in the hardware section looking for the roof hammer he said he needed.

Martin eyed the jars of candy, but he kept his hands in his pockets so that Mr. Thoxley could see that he wasn't one of the "little raccoon bandits" just waiting for him to turn his back.

As Martin quietly waited, a woman came up to the cash register with a dozen eggs, a package of macaroons, and a box of corn-pads. Mr. Thoxley leaned forward and spoke to the woman in a slightly quieter voice: "Good morning, Miss Meeks. Do you think these little boys that come in here hope that Maynard T. Thoxley is getting old and too slow to catch them?"

"Why Mr. Thoxley," the woman said kindly, "you're not getting old. Why you're...you're...young at heart! That's what you are, Mr. Thoxley."

"That's right!" he said so quickly that he snapped Miss Meeks' head back a little. "Mr. Thoxley has plenty of heart," he said pointing to his chest, "and more than a few tablespoons of honey in his disposition and just enough vinegar to get him out of bed and get his legs moving every day. After all, I've got a *business* to run here!"

As the kindly woman left with her purchase, Martin took a deep breath and stepped up to the counter. He cleared his voice: "I'll have a bag of the horehound candy, please."

Mr. Thoxley leaned forward and gave Martin kind of a hard glance, but Martin held his ground. Mr. Thoxley slowly took out a small white bag, dipped the scoop into the candy jar, filled the bag, and then held it just out of Martin's reach.

The two looked at each other for a long moment.

"Gonna pay for this?" Mr. Thoxley said a little tartly. Martin handed him two quarters. Mr. Thoxley looked at the quarters in the palm of his hand: "Not enough. This is seventy-five cents worth of candy here."

He then weighed the candy just to make sure. By that time Martin had found another quarter in the pockets of his jeans and he handed it to Mr. Thoxley. He noticed that Martin's hand was badly scarred, but he tried not to stare.

"Here, sir," Martin said, "I'm sorry I gave you the wrong amount."

Mr. Thoxley almost smiled, but he did his best to stifle it. He took another long look at Martin, and then he said something surprising: "Well, here's a little man who pays his bills, and he's a gentleman on top of it. Sorry to snap at you, young fellow. Tell you what, I'll give you two half-bags of whatever candy you want here. How about that?"

Nonie was just then reaching the register. She had two paperbacks in hand, both from the series of "Old Bombery" stories about an elderly and slightly frumpy English detective who lives in a treehouse and eats only sausages, grilled cheese sandwiches, and a few oak leaves as a garnish.

"Why, Mr. Thoxley," Nonie said, "what a sweet thing you're doing for our Martin!"

Mr. Thoxley's face relaxed even more and he cleared his voice: "Maynard T. Thoxley is not a mean man. Lord knows he gives away more candy than he sells. The rest...well, the rest gets *stolen*. Oh, well," he added, his voice dropping, "I guess I made my point on that."

Next, Papa Cider came to the counter with his roof hammer, while Mr. Thoxley filled one bag with lemon drops and another with butterscotch.

"Well, thank you for these sweet treats, Mr. Thoxley!" Papa Cider thundered so loud that Mr. Thoxley put his finger to his lips to quiet him, probably because he didn't want the rest of the store to know he was giving out free candy.

"We'll have plenty of candy for the ride home, won't we, Nonie?" Martin said cheerfully.

"Well, I guess you *will*," Mr. Thoxley said smiling cheerfully, his mood now so completely changed that he seemed truly baffled by his own sudden happiness.

Papa Cider paid for his hammer and as they all headed out, Nonie called back from the doorway: "Thank you again, Mr. Thoxley. You truly are a kind man."

"Always kind and even-tempered and...oh, well," he answered back as he returned to his work, "I guess everyone knows that by now."

Martin was very quiet on the ride home as he thought about something.

"Why do grown-ups get that way? Kind of sad and mad at the same time?" Martin asked just as a light summer rain began hitting the windshield of the car.

"Well," Papa Cider said, "Maybe for some folks, life doesn't turn out the way they wanted. And sometimes they become a little disappointed in themselves."

"He was really nice to me," Martin said.

"Yes, he was," Nonie added as she took a long look at Martin who leaned forward from the back seat. "You bring that out in people, Martin. It's a real gift."

Martin took a deep breath: "I like Mr. Thoxley. And just look at all the candy he gave us."

On the ride home, they each sampled some of the candy from the different bags. Eventually, Papa Cider settled on the lemon drops which he said were "nice and pucker-ish." Nonie liked the sweet butterscotch. For Martin, it was the horehound that was best.

CHAPTER SIXTEEN

It was about 10:30 the next morning when Martin brought his binoculars to the beach and looked out to the lake. He spotted a small flotilla of animals moving across the rough water and toward the beach at Three Tamaracks. There was a white goose gliding over the surface of the lake. Every few yards it would rise out of the water as if drying its wings. There was black on the tips of the otherwise white wings, so this told Martin that it was a snow goose he was seeing.

Also in the water, not too far from the snow goose, Martin could make out the figure of an otter that moved smartly through the water. He would occasionally dive and then rise up again and turn over to swim on his back. He seemed to like to squirt water through his small sharp teeth in the direction of the snow goose who would, in turn, let out a series of what sounded like angry honks.

Near the snow goose and the otter, Martin could see the tiny figure of Myra scrambling in the deep water. Her legs were busy as she tried her best to keep up with the other two who moved quickly across the morning waves. Every once in a while, the otter would drop down under the water, rise up and flip Myra in the air as if she were a little toy.

When this happened Martin could hear the very small but distinct voice of Myra crying out in protest: "You...you...you *stop* that, Cheevis!" Myra was clearly not amused by the antics of the otter.

"Oh," Martin said to himself as he lowered his binoculars, "this is going to be a lively morning. Myra has brought her friends!"

Not a moment later, the three creatures were on the beach. First out of the water was the otter who shook his very shiny coat. He had a small head, alert eyes, and a swath of beige across his otherwise brown face. He also had long luxurious whiskers that looked a bit like a drooping mustache: "Hi, Kid. I'm Cheevis. Some would say I'm pretty handsome."

He stretched his long neck, raised his very shapely little head, and looked up at Martin: "I don't think I'm all *that* handsome, but what do you think?"

Martin was a little taken aback. He was used to hearing Myra speak a few words at a time, but now he was seeing creatures who spoke much as people did, and it was a little unsettling. He knew that Papa Cider and Nonie heard nothing when Myra spoke. How could he explain to them, or anyone else, about an otter who spoke almost as well as any person you might meet?

The next out of the water was the snow goose. She flapped the moisture out of her wings and waddled with thick-webbed feet up to Martin: "Pay no attention to Cheevis. He's *always* fishing for compliments. Two worst things you can do with an otter is give him a ball or hand him a compliment—he'll run away with both of them, I tell you."

"And what's your name?" Martin asked politely.

"Florelle," the snow goose answered smartly. "I'm told the name has something to do with flowers. That's me—all sunny days and flowers, I am."

"Oh, wow," Cheevis said, shaking his head. "Did I hear that right? Sun and flowers? Why if she isn't the mopiest goose ever, I don't know who is."

"*Dopey?*' Is *that* what you said?'" Florelle was so sputtering mad that she raised her wings and dropped her head as if she were ready to charge Cheevis who shrunk down and closed his eyes as he braced to get his head pecked by Florelle's rather large orange beak.

"You see? You see?" Cheevis said, looking up at Martin, "Why, she's just an angry thatch of water-repellant feathers... and I SWEAR she's about to attack, so everyone head for the hills! Mad goose! Mad goose! Everybody run!!"

But Florelle wasn't about to attack anyone. She had calmed down by now and her feathers were unruffled, and she kept her head high and dignified: "Patience. I must have patience. Yes, he's an annoying, twisty little otter, but I can stay above all that." She took a deep sigh: "Oh, friendship can be a trial at times—especially when your friend is a wise-cracking little *mud-thumper* like this one."

Cheevis sidled up to Martin and whispered so Florelle wouldn't hear: "You see, she's much happier when she's mad. Had a sad childhood so she gets really mopey. She was blown off course when she was a little nipper and ended up in these mountains. Never saw her family again.

Sad, very sad goose. She gets a little *snippy* if not a little *snipey* too...and watch out when she lowers her head and starts sputtering. That's when she goes 'mad goose' on you, and you might as well just say your prayers."

By this time Myra, who was off to the side, was laughing very hard. It sounds like a string of little burps and sneezes and farts when a turtle laughs.

Cheevis now nudged Martin by rubbing his face against the bottom of his pant legs: "Hey, Martin. Did I tell you about the large vocabulary I have? Not a word in the world I don't know."

"Outrageous, isn't he?" Florelle snapped, "What an annoying little otter!"

"Well, how about it, Kid? Toss me a word and see if I don't know it."

Cheevis' eyes were so bright and intent that Martin felt he better play along. He knew that otters were fun-loving animals, but he never imagined that it had anything to do with words.

So, he paused for a second, but couldn't think of a word. Should it be a hard word? That might be unfair. He glanced along the path that led back to the cottage and he spotted a holly bush with red berries and prickers.

"All right, Mr. Cheevis. I have a word for you and the word is 'holly.'"

"Oh, too easy!" Cheevis scoffed. "Why everyone knows Holly. She's a beaver who lives down at the Big Marsh. She's been seen a lot with Gustavus Chubb lately. They must be in love. They just sit near their beaver lodge and smile at each other with those big orange bucky teeth of theirs."

"Um, no," Martin said. "I don't think you're under-standing exactly what ...."

"No more!" Florelle cried out. "No more orange teeth! Why every time Cheevis talks I feel like there's a little chig-ger eating away at my brain."

Martin then looked over to where Myra was still laugh-ing so hard—again with that series of little sneezy sounds—that she had toppled over onto her back and her little legs were flailing helplessly in the air.

Immediately Cheevis leaped over to where she lay with her shell on the sand, and he used his snout to flip her back over until she was upright.

"Thank you, Cheevis," Martin said. "That was quick work on your part. Myra hates to be upside down."

Now Cheevis moved closer to Martin and out of earshot of Myra. "You know," he said, "Myra's a little...*slow*...if you know what I mean."

Martin shook his head. He was pretty sure what Cheevis was getting at, but he wasn't having any of it.

"Myra," he said looking down on the turtle, "would you mind if I lift you up for a second?"

Myra said nothing. Martin knew it would be all right, so he lifted her up for everyone to see. He held her straight up and down so her head was at the top, her short tail be-low. He then pointed to the beautiful hard yellow plastron that covers the underside of a turtle like Myra.

"See this?" he said, turning to Cheevis and Florelle. "Do you know what's inside of this shell?"

"Turtle soup!" Cheevis said, trying his best not to laugh at his own joke.

Martin shot him a scolding look, "No, Cheevis. What's inside of this turtle's armor is a heart, an enormous heart.

Why it's a heart as big as this lake, as big as the sky. It's a heart so big it's fed by all the brooks and rivers all over these Adirondack Mountains."

By now Cheevis and Florelle were quiet and fascinated.

"What would you say about a baby turtle who was wounded and paddled her way across the lake and found the people who could help her heal? What would you say about a turtle who lives at night in the Big Marsh but finds her way here each day because she knows she has a friend waiting? I'd call that heart."

"Hooray!" Florelle, who could not contain herself anymore, cried out. "What a speech! Hooray for Myra!"

Cheevis hung his head and looked a little embarrassed. "I *only* said she was a little slow."

"She's slow," Martin continued, "because she wants to take her time and take in all the pretty things in the world. Everything she does is full of heart. What a turtle you are, Myra!"

With that Martin carefully set Myra back down in the sand.

"Well, she *is* a sweetie," Cheevis said, "and I never said she wasn't."

CHAPTER SEVENTEEN

The banter went on like that for a while until there was the sound of footsteps coming down the stone path leading to the beach. All of the gathered animals went silent at once. Martin was especially surprised at how fast a chatty otter like Cheevis could become so quiet so quickly, and how Florelle could pretend to be pecking at the beach sand just like any wild snow goose looking for a little bite to eat.

Nonie stepped onto the beach wearing a broad straw sun bonnet to protect her fair skin.

She must have been working on one of her paintings because she had on the light-blue smock she wore when she painted her nature scenes. She seemed not at all surprised to be seeing an otter and a snow goose on the beach. Geese of various kinds and otters were fairly common around Orenda Lake.

She turned first to Florelle: "Well, look at you, miss. Aren't you just a fine species of snow goose!"

With that, she reached into the pocket of her smock and brought out a pack of crackers wrapped in cellophane.

She then crushed them until they were crumbs and stepped up to the shallow water near the beach. She tossed the crumbs out into the shallow water where Florelle quickly snapped them up with her broad bill.

Nonie then turned to Cheevis. "I'm not sure I have anything for you to eat, but I must say you're an alert-looking fellow with a lovely head. What a handsome otter you are!"

Cheevis closed his eyes in pleasure—he clearly loved being flattered.

Nonie then took off her sunbonnet and shook her long, luxurious red-and-silver hair in the clean breeze coming off the lake. "Ah, such a day!" she said. "Part of me wants to paint or draw and part of me just wants to linger on this beach, but I must go! Places are calling to me; places and scenes and flowers that want to be painted and remembered. Goodbye, my friends." With that, she was heading back to the cabin to pick up her paint box and easel.

Once she was gone, Cheevis immediately turned to the others: "Did you hear that? She said I was handsome. Hey, I'm sort of moved by that, I really am."

"Outrageous!" Florelle cried out. "Stop your preening, you silly otter. You see, Martin, what I put up with? Always fish-fish-fishing for compliments. Let's just get on our way, Cheevis."

Myra didn't follow them but stayed near Martin as Cheevis and Florelle entered the water and began to swim out onto the lake.

In an instant Cheevis was floating on his back, his beige belly showing, and he called back to Martin: "Hey, Kid! You never gave me a hard word. Come on, toss me a word...and don't make it too easy this time, eh?"

Martin thought to himself that it was time that Cheevis be put in his place, so he searched his mind for a word that might be a bit of a challenge to his new friend, a playful but surly otter.

The previous night Martin had been reading another book, this one called *The Strange and Wonderful Creatures of Australia and New Zealand.* He'd read in the book about a strange little mammal called a Duck-billed Platypus that had a snout like a duck's bill, a flat tail like a beaver, webbed feet and it even laid eggs.

"Come on, Kid," Cheevis persisted, "give me a word."

"Okay," Martin answered, "here's your word: platy-pus."

Cheevis stopped in the water. He looked a little shocked: "Platter-platter...what?"

"Pla-ty-pus," Martin continued, now sounding out the word carefully.

"Oh, I know what a platter-puss is," Cheevis said, "but I don't think it's a very *nice* word to be calling somebody, and I happen to be in a hurry now, so bye-bye."

With that, he did a quick flip, dived under the water, and disappeared.

"Stumped him!" Florelle called out to Martin. "Why he has no idea what platter-puss even means...not the froggi-est idea! Isn't it a ton of fun to stump an otter?"

Florelle then paddled out into the water and when she was about a hundred yards out, Cheevis again resurfaced and the two bickered away at each other until they swam out of sight.

Martin sat down cross-legged in the sand right next to Myra. He shook his head and laughed at the idea that these two creatures, a snow goose, and an otter, were friends who clearly irritated each other, but they also seemed kind of close and devoted.

"Fun-ny!" Myra said, craning her long neck as she turned and looked up at Martin.

"Yes," Martin said, "your two friends *are* funny, Myra, and those are the best types of friends to have...ones that are funny. I'm awfully glad you have friends down at the Big Marsh."

"And here!" Myra said cheerfully.

"Yep, Myra, you'll always have a friend right here."

That night as he lay in bed and thought about the day, he knew one thing: ever since he'd met Myra, he was happier than ever before. He might never be able to explain to anyone that he was able to converse with Myra and an otter and a snow goose. Ever since Papa Cider that day a summer ago had told him to listen to the animals, he was hearing many of them clearly now, and they were a part of his life. He also knew that one day he would grow older and might not be able to talk with creatures anymore. Still, he truly loved all the animals, including the silent ones.

So, for now, he was living out an adventure at Three Tamaracks. These were summers he would always remember, and who knew what still lay ahead of him? He had at least a little bit of his boyhood left, and he knew he should never wish it away.

CHAPTER EIGHTEEN

Martin and Nonie had wondered why Papa Cider wanted to paddle a boat out into Orenda Lake so late at night, but now they knew—it was a full moon. The moon-light was so bright it shone on the mountains around the lake, and it looked like all the pines and broad-leaf trees were skimmed with newly fallen snow.

Papa Cider knew that a windless, full-moon night in summer was the best time to row. He had brought his prized Adirondack guide boat out of the boathouse. It was made of wood and had a polished look. It appeared at first glance like a canoe but was flatter on the bottom and was wider in the middle. The design was thought to be based on boats the Mohawk Indians once made out of wood and tree bark. Adirondack fishing guides once used the boats in an earlier age to take people to the best places to fish on lakes like Orenda.

Instead of paddles, the boat had oars like a rowboat, and Papa Cider sat in a seat that had a raised back to lean into as he smoothly pulled the oars through the very still night water. Once in a while, Papa Cider would say, in a whisper, "Be still now...be still to keep 'er steady. Listen...just listen." Martin and Nonie were as still and quiet as possible in their seats in the front and back of the guide boat.

And so, they all simply listened to the sound of the water as the oars pulled, and eddies in the water looked like little swirls of moonlight. The lights inside many of the cabins on the shore of Orenda Lake reflected on the still surface of the water, and they could smell the pine-wood smoke from the fireplaces in cabins that ringed the long lake.

"Keep still now," Papa Cider repeated, and he stopped rowing and pulled up the oars for a second as they all heard one loon sound its trilling call from the east end of the lake, and an answer came from another loon somewhere near the lake's west bay.

Martin looked over the side of the boat. The moonlight was so bright that he could see the shadow of the boat moving along the lake's sandy bottom. He had no idea what time it might be or how long they'd been out on the boat, but he wasn't a bit tired. Even though he was only eleven years old, he knew that he was living out a night he would never forget.

Papa Cider started rowing again, very slowly now. He cleared his voice before speaking.

"The next few days Nonie will teach you to row this boat. She'll also take you out so you can learn to use the kayaks. There are two of them. I made them myself out of cedar wood. You'll have to be careful with them."

"Thanks, Papa Cider. They're pretty nice kayaks, and I'll sure be careful with them."

"Nonie will teach you because she's a better kayaker than me, but I'll give you lessons too."

Now he lifted the oars up again into the boat, and they just drifted quietly.Martin looked directly up at the moon, which was so bright it almost made his eyes hurt. He had a question in mind, but he was sure it would be hard to answer. He then pointed up to the moon.

"Anyone up there? I heard thunder once, and it sounded like a voice. "

Nonie and Papa Cider looked at each other

"By golly," Cider said, "that's one big question for an eleven-year-old."

"But what do you think, Papa Cider?"

"Well," he said, as he rubbed his face, "I guess I don't think of it that way if you're talking about some far-away God living up high. Just assumed that if there's a God, must be right here...everywhere, I guess...right now, right here."

Nonie turned toward Martin. Her hair was lit by the moon, so much so that it looked almost golden-white to Martin, and it shone so bright he could barely see the features of her face.

"What do you think, Martin?"

Martin hesitated. He dropped his head and then lifted it, and Papa and Nonie could see his clear green eyes, intensely focused, in the evening light.

"I think Papa Cider's right," he said as he turned his head and looked around the lake and saw reflections of the mountains on the still water, "right here, right now."

CHAPTER NINETEEN

It had reached the point in August when it was time again to close the cabin, take the chairs off the porch and the beach, and say goodbye to another summer at "Three Tamaracks." In the boat house, the guide boat and two wooden kayaks were lifted onto a rack where they would sit up high over the winter. Papa Cider brought out the plywood sheets that would cover the windows.

As Papa Cider and Nonie cleaned the rooms, even the empty chairs, the couch, and tables looked solitary and alone as the people who used them were about to leave. In a few short months, the camp would be taken over by deer, raccoons, chipmunks, and the ever-present crows who stayed the winter and called from the tops of trees. Ice would spread over the lake and blizzards would blow heavy snows over the dens and holes of animals safely burrowed from storms.

Far down at the south side of the lake, ice would cover the Big Marsh, and Myra, driven by the need to survive the harsh winter, would find her place deep down in the mud and go into a long sleep. In time she would rise again in spring where she might sit on a log on a warm day and wonder if it were time to again visit her friend at Three Tamaracks.

On his last vacation day on the beach of Three Tamaracks, Martin arrived early and was surprised at what he found. Myra had arrived earlier than usual and was part of a circle that included Florelle and Cheevis. The three of them were in a deep discussion although it was Florelle and Cheevis who seemed to do all the talking while Myra, her neck stretched, listened intently to the other two.

It was unusual for Martin to see Myra this early in the morning and to hear Florelle and Cheevis in such a serious discussion and not the usual bantering at each other. Florelle seemed too distracted by what they were saying to be annoyed by Cheevis.

"Well," Martin said cheerfully, "good morning, to all of you!"

Cheevis, who had been deep in discussion, looked a little startled, but Myra merely looked up at Martin with that little smile she always seemed to have. Florelle lifted her wings to dry off the last bit of water left on her feathers.

"Dry your wings later, Florelle," Cheevis said a little tartly. "We have *serious* things to talk about here. No use pecking around. We might as well get right to it."

Just before speaking, Cheevis gave a last shake of his sleek coat that threw a little water on everyone including Martin.

"Outrageous!" Florelle said, "isn't he outrageous? No manners at all!"

Cheevis ignored the remark and turned directly to

Martin: "Kid, do you know how to use the boat in there?" Cheevis nodded toward the boat house.

"You mean the guide boat?" Martin asked.

"Is that what it's called?"

"Yes, it's Papa Cider's guide boat. I *am* learning to use it right now. It's a little tricky, but I'm learning from Nonie and Papa Cider. Nonie learned to row in college."

"College?" Cheevis said, looking a little confused. "Oh, well, I do *actually* know that word. It's just not coming to me right now...but listen, Kid. Could you handle that boat well enough to make it up Bender Creek?"

"Bender Creek?" Martin said as he scratched the tousled mop of hair on his head and thought for a second. "Why, Bender Creek is a little dangerous. It has rapids, and it has quick twists and turns and lots of big rocks, right?"

"Right," Cheevis answered, "and do you know where the Creek goes?"

"Yep," Martin said, "it ends at Glacier Pond, or, I guess you could say, it *begins* at Glacier Pond."

Now it was Florelle's turn to speak: "And you know who's at Glacier Pond, don't you?"

"Oh, wait a minute," Martin said, as it was all dawning on him now. "Nonie told me that the Piebald Deer lives around Glacier Pond."

"Yep, that's right, Kid," Cheevis continued, "and when you see the big Piebald Deer, something wonderful always happens."

"Like what?" Martin asked.

"Oh, I can't tell you that, Kid. It's different for everyone, but it's always wonderful."

"Well, I'll have to give it a go!"

Cheevis let out a cheer, Florelle let out a series of happy

goose-honks, and Myra opened her mouth wide as she tried to cheer, but it was a little too much for her, so no sound came out except for a little belch—but she *did* look very happy.

"But wait a minute," Martin said doubtfully. "I'm just learning to use the guide boat, and I wouldn't want to wreck it. Bender Creek has all those rapids and rocks, and when I think of how it bends and turns all over the place...well, I don't know. It's hard. And I'd be rowing *up-stream*."

"Of course, it's hard, Kid. That's just the point. You might have to learn to fight your way up the current some time. Why not try? You've got the whole winter to think about it, and you could practice your rowing at the beginning of the summer and wait until the end of the summer to try Bender Creek."

"Or," Martin answered, "I could practice next summer and try Bender Creek the following summer!"

All the gathered animals fell silent at this suggestion. Martin looked at them all.

"What's the matter with taking a little time to get myself ready?"

"Time," Cheevis said.

"Time," Florelle repeated.

"Time," Myra said with her tiny little voice, but she was a little confused as she looked at the other two. "Time?" she now asked as if she wasn't exactly certain what they were talking about.

"Time's what we don't have a lot of, Kid," Cheevis said as his head dropped sadly.

When Martin realized what they were actually talking

about, he felt a catch in his throat and almost felt like crying. He remembered at that moment what short lives otters and geese and so many other animals have. Of all the creatures he could think of around the lake, it was only turtles like Myra who had lives as long as the lives of most people. If he were to wait too long Cheevis and Florelle might not be around to see his trip to Glacier Pond, and it seemed very important to them.

Martin knew what he had to do, but first, he had to solve something in his mind as he pictured going up the creek: "No. It can't be the guide boat. I'd be rowing upstream against the current. My back would be to the current, and I'd have to look over my shoulder to see what was ahead. That wouldn't work. But I do know what *would* work: I could go upstream with one of Papa Cider's kayaks. That way I could maneuver better, holding one kayak paddle and just digging into the water on each side to make sure I can steer out to the rapids. That just might work. Okay, now that I've solved that problem, I know I *am* going to do it!"

Immediately Myra said: "I want to go!"

"And you will, Myra. You'll ride in the kayak with me. It'll be tight, but I'll figure out a way. Are the two of you going?"

"Wouldn't miss it," Cheevis said.

"Me either," Florelle added, " but I might have to fly part of the way. I don't like to paddle through fast waters. No goose in her right mind...."

"Then it's settled," Cheevis said. "We're all going up Bender Creek next summer to see the Piebald Deer, right?"

"Right," Florelle said.

"Right," Martin repeated.

"Me too!" Myra said.

Martin watched as Florelle and Cheevis departed. He would keep his promise, and the next summer he knew would be a time of adventure. At the same time, he knew that Nonie and Cider would never let him paddle up Bender Creek alone. He didn't like the idea of lying to them. It would be the first time he'd ever defied them this way. But he felt it might be the right time to try something a little defiant, to go his own way, to paddle a kayak up a twisting and tricky river. And Bender Creek *was* wide as a river, and its rocks and rapids had no special love for little boys or girls.

It would be a dangerous trip, and it would test him. The trip might just *break* him but knew he might need that. Things from the past still gnawed at him, especially at night when he was alone. Maybe he needed to break a little and then put himself together again. Maybe Cheevis and Florelle knew this. Was it possible? Were they even wiser than he thought?

The sky that afternoon had grown dark. Martin sat on a smooth driftwood log on the beach and Myra sat quietly at his feet. He looked up at dark swelling clouds in the sky and he could feel the coming of a thunderstorm, so he didn't want to keep Myra too long, but he knew he must choose his words carefully because another summer had ended. He'd have to leave his turtle friend once again and head for home. He took a deep breath before he spoke.

"Myra," he said, "it's that time. The summer's come to an end, and we'll have to say goodbye...again."

Myra's eyes blinked as she looked up at him. He bent over and lifted her onto his lap.

She looked out at the water of the lake and then re-peated Martin's word: "Good...bye."

"Do you understand that word now, Myra?"

"I...understand," she said, and Martin knew that it was true; he could tell by the sad way that she said it.

"Every year at this time, we have to say goodbye, and it will always hurt."

"Hurts," she said and then paused for a moment and said it again, "hurts."

"But if we have to keep saying goodbye every year, that's a good thing, Myra. It means we'll have a lot of summers together, maybe even until we're old."

"Old?" Myra said. She didn't seem to understand the concept yet. She wasn't quite two years old after all. "Are we...old?" she asked sweetly.

"Not yet, Myra. But I do hope we *will* be someday because that will mean we've had a lot of years behind us and that would be a wonderful thing."

They sat there on the log for a while and neither wanted to move. Finally, Martin lifted Myra up and looked at her. Then he set her down on the sand and kissed his hand and touched it to her shell.

There was a rumble of thunder and Martin looked up at the sky. "Time for you to make your way back to the Big Marsh, Myra. I'll give you a boost."

With that Martin lifted her as he stepped into the shallow water of the lake. He set her down in the rippling water and immediately her little legs began to move, and she started to swim away.

"Goodbye, Myra...and remember: I'll see you next summer, no matter what."

Soon she was off into the waves. Martin looked up at

the dark sky again. He hoped Myra would make it back to the Big Swamp before the lightning started. He knew that when he got into Papa Cider's car and traveled the road home he'd be thinking about her.

CHAPTER TWENTY

When he returned to his hometown school that year the courses were getting harder, and his homework took longer. He loved the old school building that had high windows that looked out on a lawn that had a statue of the famous Seneca Indian chief named Red Jacket whose tribe was native to the area Martin lived in.

Martin looked forward to some of his classes, particularly science classes and especially when they focused on the plants and animals. Martin turned in a paper about Painted Turtles that won the "Irving Howitt Award" given to the best science essay from a seventh-grader. Martin had several friends, and he was increasingly noticing the girls around him, but there was one thing that occupied his mind more than any other—his journey up Bender Creek in the coming summer.

In study halls, while the other kids were working on assignments or bantering back and forth, Martin studied one of Papa Cider's old hiking maps of the areas around Orenda Lake. His eyes would follow the jagged line of one particular creek on the map. He studied the long curves and sharp bends in the creek—no wonder they called it "Bender" Creek. He also imagined the white-water rapids he was likely to encounter. Then his eyes would follow the line of the creek up to where it began, the small lake called "Glacier Pond." Even on a map it looked cool and still, the place where Bender Creek began. Each time he was finished with the map, studying it for maybe the tenth time that day, he folded it neatly, put it in his pocket, and said, "Time to meet the Piebald Deer. Here I come."

When Martin returned to Three Tamaracks the following summer, he immediately threw himself into continuing to learn how to paddle and maneuver one of Papa Cider's custom-made wooden kayaks. Sometimes Nonie, who was in the other kayak beside him, provided the lessons; sometimes it was Papa Cider. They were both good teachers who gave Martin firm, crisp instructions about efficiently using the single paddle used to propel and steer a kayak. The only problem was that Papa Cider was losing his hearing a little, so Martin sometimes felt like he was being yelled at when he was next to him, but he knew Papa was only trying to help.

Between the two of his parents, Martin learned the best way to grip the single paddle used for a kayak. He learned how to make the blades of the paddle propel him smoothly forward. He learned a reverse stroke that might come in handy when it was time to deal with the strong current at Bender Creek. He also learned what Nonie called the "sweep stroke" for turning the kayak. He seemed to have a good feel for the kayaks, and he picked up the different maneuvers quickly.

Through the course of the kayak lessons, Martin thought of how generous Nonie and Papa Cider were in helping him. Always at the back of his mind was the thought that they had no idea he was going to use his kayak skills to take him up Bender Creek.

Soon Martin had achieved enough skill that Nonie and Papa Cider were allowing him to practice on his own farther out in Orenda Lake, but only if he wore a safety jacket and stayed away from the areas of the lake where the big power boats roared and left steep wakes in the water. It was hard work for Martin to be paddling the kayak every day under the hot sun, and he often sweated through a few T-shirts. He could feel that he was growing his young muscles and developing the stamina he would need for that day in August when he would try to paddle his way up Bender Creek.

When he returned to the beach after a few hours of rowing, he'd usually find Myra napping in the shade underneath a blueberry bush. For the third summer in a row, she'd found her way back to him. She was now at full-size for a Painted Turtle—about ten inches long from nose to tail. Her shell was darker than before and had a bright, polished sheen, especially when the sun struck it directly. Myra was truly a pretty turtle especially to those who appreciate the special beauty of a turtle.

Most importantly for Martin, Myra was still very much the sweet turtle she'd always been. She still spoke only a little, and when she spoke, it was always direct and from the heart. Not a word was wasted.

When Martin was out practicing in the kayak, he tried to make it back to the beach in time to have lunch with Myra (sandwiches for him, and fruit and meal worms for

Myra), but he was worried that he was not spending enough time with her. He had to think of a way to bring her along when he paddled while not letting her get too hot or dry as she sat in the bottom of the kayak.

Finally, he began bringing Myra along on his paddling voyages. It was only fair after all. Myra spent a long time each morning traveling across the lake from the Big Marsh to Three Tamaracks. It was her purpose each day to see her friend who spoke with her and had once nursed her back to health. It's always hard to tell about a turtle's memory, but Myra seemed to remember the acts of kindness she'd received. She'd always be devoted to Martin.

On the first day he took Myra out in the kayak, it was a hot, cloudless, sun-glaring day. Martin placed Myra on a damp towel in the bottom of the kayak in a small space in front of the seat and between his two legs. He provided a tiny saucer of water and a small paper plate with bits of fruit and finely cut lettuce. He thought this would keep her cool and happy, but it was still very hot in the bottom of the kayak. As Martin rowed, he'd glance down to make sure Myra was not getting overheated.

At one point Myra seemed as if she were drying out too much and might be getting over- heated so Martin paused from his paddling, reached over the side of the boat, and scooped up some lake water in his hand, and doused Myra with the cold water. Myra might have been napping because she was startled by the cold water: "Hey...hey...hey...you *stop* that, Martin!"

"I'm just trying to keep you cool, Myra." Martin could see that Myra was a little indignant and saw the splash of water as a nasty trick. Martin could also see that setting Myra in the bottom of the kayak, where she could see nothing, was not the best arrangement. After thinking about it for a few seconds, he had the answer: "Myra, how about a swim?"

"Swim," Myra said very happily, in fact so happily that she kept repeating her favorite word: "Oh, swim...I'll swim... and, and you, Martin?"

"Not for me right now, Myra, but here you go." He lifted her up from the bottom of the kayak and placed her in the lake. Her little legs begin moving even before she touched the water. Once in the water, those little legs and webbed feet went to work, and she began to motor happily over the waves. As Martin watched her, he marveled at the thought of how those little legs brought her through big waves and over high boat wakes, and through storms and heavy rain, as each morning of summer she made the daily journey from the Big Marsh.

Weeks passed and Martin paddled and paddled some more, sometimes for up to three hours a day. He had grown to love the kayak with its gleaming varnished cedarwood finish. He found he had to wear gloves because the scar tissue on his left hand could break open and bleed. Sometimes when he felt his hands stinging inside the gloves, he'd try to remember how his hand, arm, and trunk had become so scarred. But no memory came back to him except how the great dark bird rescued him—but from what? He might never know.

Paddling for long stretches of time gave him time to think. He often tried to imagine what Bender Creek was like. Was it as dangerous as everyone said with roiling rapids, big rocks, and twisting turns? And was Glacier Pond as magical a place as Cheevis and Florelle described it?

Out on the lake, he also thought about what a cruel

trick he was playing on Papa Cider and Nonie. He had told them the lie that it was actually the Big Marsh that he was preparing to visit alone. He still believed that if he told them he was going to Bender Creek, they'd never say "yes" to such a dangerous trip.

It was strange for him to think about how he was trusting the word of a comical, somewhat silly otter and his companion, a short-tempered snow goose. When they said that "something wonderful" would happen when he saw the Piebald Deer at Glacier Pond, he believed them. He also remembered Nonie's stories about the Piebald Deer, so there was no doubt he had to take his journey.

He knew deep down that the journey would be a big event in his life. He had to do it, and he told himself that one day in the future he would come clean and tell Papa Cider and Nonie about the whole trip, and how he'd lied to them. He knew he'd be forgiven after a time because they were forgiving people. After all, how could they deny a boy who wanted to brave the rapids and maybe see the big stag, the Piebald Deer? Now it was up to him to reach his destination—with the help of some animal friends.

CHAPTER TWENTY-ONE

August came around, and the day had arrived for Martin's trip. The Monday he'd chosen was cloudless and the clear air was just cool enough. In front of the small dock of the boat house, Martin sat making his last adjustments to the foot pedals inside the kayak. Papa Cider stood on the dock looking down at him and at one point squatted down and reached out to tighten the straps and buckles on Martin's life jacket.

Nonie paced nervously on the dock. Martin was ready to go, so he put on a green baseball cap that had a white "O" on the front of it, above the brim. He then put on a pair of aviator sunglasses. "All right," he whispered to himself, "I'm ready."

Nonie and Papa Cider were quiet as they made the last preparations before a trip they thought would be taking Martin to the Big Marsh. Nonie handed him two canteens of cold water and an old-fashioned child's lunch box that had little songbirds painted on it.

Martin raised his sunglasses and opened the lunch box

and then smiled up at Nonie who stood above him on the dock.

"Hmm. Looks like brownies," he said happily. "And these sandwiches...cream cheese and olive maybe?"

"No, peanut butter and fresh honey, Martin. It will give you plenty of energy, and you'll need it." She paused and shook her head and muttered, "Oh, my, my! I just don't know about this."

Martin looked up at Papa Cider who stood with his hands on his hips as he surveyed the prized wooden kayak he had made with his own hands. Martin had noticed how this summer Papa Cider looked a little more stooped, older, a little slower in his motions. But there always was that relaxed and gentle look in his watchful eyes, no matter what was going on at the time.

Nonie repeated something she'd said earlier: "You know the two of us could take the guide boat or canoe and follow you down to the Big Marsh."

"Nope, nope," Papa Cider said shaking his head, "The boy wants to try it alone, Nonie. Now if we're going to worry, I'll sit next to you on the porch and we'll worry together. That'd be more than fine with me, but there's no stopping Martin from taking this trip."

"Well, all right then, go ahead, Martin," Nonie said, "but if you're not back by 4:30, I swear I'll call out the Orenda Lake rescue squad to look for you, and I *mean* it."

Martin smiled at her. "Just have to test myself, Nonie."

"So let's get you started, Martin," Papa Cider said excitedly, "I'll give you a good push to get you off to a good start."

"Just one more thing," Martin said, his tight-gloved hands on the paddle. "Myra may be by soon. Would you check in on her today? I really shouldn't bring her along in the kayak. Not much room."

"Will do," Papa Cider said, and he waded into the water so that his pants were wet up to the waist. He got behind the back of the kayak and gave a mighty push and Martin was off. He began to work the paddle as one blade of the paddle rose high, while the other cut through the water. He kept the circular motions of the paddle going in almost perfect synchronization until he found his rhythm and the kayak began to take on speed.

"Goodbye!" he said.

Papa Cider yelled back, his voice carrying over the water as Martin got farther and farther from the shore: "I got the feeling this is a journey you won't soon forget, son!" He cupped his hands and yelled louder, "We'll be waiting right here for you—at your home."

CHAPTER TWENTY-TWO

Martin was putting his effort into the paddling and was moving along smartly. When he was about 200 yards from the shore he looked off to the side and saw Myra paddling her short little legs through the water as she headed in the opposite direction. Martin tried to sit a bit lower as if he could pass Myra without her noticing—that didn't work out so well.

Myra, her neck stretched and her little head above the water, knew the kayak when she saw it. She did a quick turn in the water and headed toward Martin. In no time she was swimming furiously, with all her might, as she trailed the boat.

Martin stopped paddling and tried to look surprised as his turtle friend drew nearer: "Oh, hi, Myra."

Myra looked straight up at Martin and her little, tiny eyes made contact with his.

"Where, where are you going, Martin?"

"Oh well, Myra," Martin said, a little tongue-tied. "I'm heading for Bender Creek. I know you thought you were going along with me, but you see, it's a little tight in here."

"I *am* going," Myra said. "I'm going with you to...Ben-Ben...Bendy Cricket."

"Bender Creek," Martin corrected her. "But it's dangerous, Myra. I thought about it. If we hit some rapids on the creek, you could get tossed around. You could end up on your *back.*"

Martin knew how much Myra hated being on her back, but he could also see it wasn't likely to discourage her.

As Myra treaded water next to the boat, she summoned all her strength to tell Martin what she thought: "Wherever Martin...goes...Myra goes!" This seemed to sum it all up for her.

Martin let out a sigh and then reached his arm out into the water and lifted Myra into the boat: "You are a *stubborn* little turtle, Myra. Are all turtles as stubborn as you are?"

He reached behind him in the boat and lifted up a box and placed it in front of him. Somehow, he knew all along that Myra might find him, so he had a box lined with soft damp towels, a little pan for Myra to drink from, a few little pieces of fresh fruit to eat.

Myra immediately got comfortable in the box. She seemed to know it would be a long trip, so she pulled her legs into her shell and closed her eyes.

Martin's long, smooth strokes of the paddle made the kayak glide across the water of Orenda Lake. It helped that there wasn't much wind that day, so the lake water was calm and unruffled. After about a half-hour Martin could see that he was approaching the place where Bender Creek emptied into the lake. He called down to Myra who was dozing.

"You'll want to wake up now, Myra. Things are going

to get bumpy pretty soon, so get ready."

There was a buoy in the water with a sign on it that said: "DANGER. ENTER AT YOUR OWN RISK. RAPID WATERS AHEAD!"

Two large, overgrown willow trees hung their branches over the water so that Martin couldn't see the mouth of the creek, but he could hear the sound of rapid waters far upstream. He paddled slowly through the thick willow branches, occasionally using the paddle to clear the branches away as his kayak moved slowly through the leafy thickets. He wondered for a second about why no one had ever trimmed these branches back, but then he realized that maybe people in the Orenda Lake community thought it was a good thing to keep the entrance to Bender Creek hidden.

Once he was past the willow branches, he found he was in almost blinding sunlight reflecting off the surface of a creek that was broad enough to be a river. He felt the current going in the opposite direction, so he had to use the paddle to steady the kayak and keep it from moving backward. He didn't immediately see any white-water rapids ahead, so he sighed in relief. Maybe there were only a few short stretches of rapids on Bender Creek, and it wasn't as hard as people had made it out to be. Or so he thought.

Martin called down to Myra who was now trying to scale the sides of her box to get a good look: "Maybe this won't be as hard as I thought, Myra."

Martin then heard the sound of wings beating and felt a shadow pass over him. He looked up and saw that it was Florelle who used her black-tipped white wings to slow herself down as she landed, gracefully skidding across the open water just ahead of the kayak.

"Hello, Florelle! Just in time! Are you going to paddle up the creek?"

"What?" Florelle said, her feathers rising a little, "*paddle*? Outrageous! Why, there are rapids up ahead. I could be crushed, *crushed* on a rock! Why, there'd be nothing left of sunny, happy Florelle but a few little feathers in the water." She sounded very sorry for herself over something that hadn't even happened. "Just a few little feathers left in the water," she repeated.

"Well, there's always another way for you, isn't there?"

"Yes. I have my wings, and I'll fly until the creek calms down a little, thank you."

"All right, that's fine, Florelle. I get what you're saying. But where is Cheevis? I thought he said he'd be here, but he's late and—"

At that very instant Cheevis, his fur wet and glistening, and his big wet mustache drooping, popped out of the water about five feet in front of the kayak.

"Late? Late? Not me, Kid. Never been late. Ready to go." He rolled on his back in the creek water and, with his chubby paws, began fussing with something on his beige belly that looked like a small crayfish.

"Oh, he's a tiresome little wiggler, isn't he?" Florelle said, but she started lifting and beating her wings in a way that made her look a little happy at Cheevis' arrival, but she was also anxious to get moving.

With one quick thrust Cheevis began a shimmying swim motion, his long, thin, muscular body turning and twisting and propelling him against the current of the creek. He stopped for a second and looked back at Martin in the boat: "I'll lead the way, Kid. I know this creek, and it can be sneaky and dangerous, so just look ahead a ways when you paddle and try to follow my lead. Got it?"

"Got it," Martin said, "but I might lose track of you."

"That's okay," Cheevis said, now starting to swim again, "just stay close to the middle of the creek where the water is deepest—and watch for the rocks! They'll come up on you pretty fast when you reach the whitewater."

Meanwhile, Florelle had now reached the muddy bank of the creek, and she spread her white wings and launched herself into the air. Martin shaded his eyes and watched her for a second as she flew above the creek. She beat her wings and sometimes slowed to a glide as she carefully followed each turn in the creek, tracing the shape of the water moving beneath her.

"Wow, Myra," Martin said, as he began pulling hard on the kayak paddle. "A snow goose flying up a river is sure a pretty sight!"

"Keep your head down and paddle" Cheevis' called back; he was now about twenty yards ahead of Martin's boat. "It's going to start getting harder pretty soon, so always keep paddling and don't let up. No time for chit-chat. It's not so hard for me, but I'm an *otter*. You're just a kid in a skinny boat, right? So get ready!"

CHAPTER TWENTY-THREE

For a while, the paddling was still not that hard for Martin. He had adjusted to paddling against the current, but the water so far was deep and gentle and there were no dangerous rocks in sight. He could even take a leisurely glance to either side and take in the scenery along the creek.

There were a few tall hemlocks along the shore that cast enough shadow to give him some relief from the sun. He passed wetland meadows with tall grasses, small ponds and deep-cutting little steams and rivulets with rust-colored water. He could see small groves of tamarack trees, their soft green needles just beginning to show a little gold because of the cold nights turning them in late summer. There were also tall, dead trees that looked like the giant upright bones of dinosaurs. The tops of a few of them had stick-thatched heron nests.

In the sky overhead, Martin could see the slow-motion wings of blue herons surveying the swamps below. High above all the other birds, Martin could see a lone golden eagle swirling far up in the bluest, clearest sky he'd ever seen.

"That's a golden eagle way up there, Myra! I think that's a sign of good luck. You don't see one of *them* every day."

Now he was coming upon a long, gradual bend in the creek, and he could feel the water getting faster, as it was shooting around the long curving bank ahead of him.

"Okay, Kid. Time to hold onto your hat once you get around this bend in the creek," Cheevis, who was even farther ahead of him now, called back. "This'll knock your freckles off."

Martin instinctively pushed down his green cap, so it was firmer on his head.

"Might lose track of each other through here, Kid. The creek wants to throw you back. It wants to guard its secrets, you see." With that Cheevis let out a loud, "WHOA, THERE," and his voice was garbled, except for the sound of one last "YIP-PEE!" as he took on the rapid waters that awaited Martin.

As Martin continued around the long curve in the creek, he found the current getting stronger. For one quick second, he kept one hand on the paddle, and with the other, he pulled Myra's box to where it would be snug between his feet and wouldn't be jostled too much.

"Hold on now, Myra—here it comes!"

"I want to see," Myra said, as she tried scaling the side of the cardboard box she was in.

"No, hold tight, Myra. Keep very low. Do you hear me? I'm not kidding around here."

With that, the front of the kayak hit the first rapids and the power of it thrust it straight backward, so Martin had to dig the paddle blades deeper into the water and he pulled hard until the kayak moved forward. Cold water splashed his face like a hard slap from the creek.

"Whoa! Now it starts to get pretty bumpy, Myra. Stay low until we get to the still waters up at Glacier Pond, okay?" He realized he was shouting now as the current got stronger and louder.

"No yell-yelling," Myra's little voice called back over the roar of the waters, but before she could finish the thought, she had pulled her head back into her shell because it *was* getting bumpy and a little scary on the wild creek.

At that very second, they hit even harder-charging rapids and the front of the kayak was lifted up by the fast current, and then it slapped down hard on the water. A spray of cold water splashed into the boat, drenching Martin's dark-green long-sleeved t-shirt and raining into Myra's box. Myra's head quickly popped out of her shell and then instantly went back into the shell again—she really didn't want to look anymore.

The kayak then suddenly dropped down in the current and Martin found he was spinning in a whirlpool in the angry creek, so he quickly and deftly switched quickly from one paddle blade to the other and steered out of the whirlpool, but he could see other hazards ahead. He thought to himself, *this creek really is as big as a river. But what does this river want from me?*

Just ahead was an enormous round rock, its smooth top just out of the water. The creek was full of rocks, some round and some upright, jagged pieces of slate. For a second, he had the horrifying picture of Papa Cider's prized wooden kayak being broken into splinters and he and

Myra being tossed into the current.

"No fun!" Myra's tiny voice called out.

By now the muscles in his arms, chest, and legs burned, and he wondered for how long he could keep digging in the paddle blades against the strong, rapid waters. The creek had straightened a bit, but it had a series of short twists and turns ahead. As soon as he'd row through one quick turn, he'd have to dig his paddle blades in deep and maneuver through another. Sometimes branches or big pieces of wood came down the creek hurtling with great speed. All the time he worked the paddle, quickly dodging each hazard in the water.

The sheer work of it left him breathless, and, in his mind, an argument was going on. One voice said *"You can't do this. Go back. Save yourself. Save Myra."*

But another calmer voice said, *"You have to make it to Glacier Pond! Something wonderful is waiting. Push onward."*

Martin gritted his teeth and continued paddling. At last, he could see ahead of him that the creek had straightened completely and what lay ahead of him was a long corridor of rapid water lined along the banks with very old, twisted trees, mostly pines.

Though it was good to be in the long, straight portion of the creek, he could see that he had far to go, and it was all white rapids ahead of him, at least a quarter of a mile of water pushing back against him. There was also an enormous old hemlock tree leaning over the creek about fifty yards ahead. Martin knew he'd have just enough room to duck his head and paddle under it. Meanwhile, it had been quite a while since he'd seen or heard from

Cheevis who probably was ahead of him somewhere facing a current that was relentless and heavy—even for a cocky otter.

Soon Martin had paddled to where the big, tilted hemlock stretched across the creek. He knew he could pass under it because it was about five feet above the water. Though it had lain across the river for many years, it had somehow held onto its life because all its needles were still green. As Martin paddled toward the bridge formed by the tree, suddenly a strong wind came up. The next thing he knew there was a sound of cracking wood.

"Myra!" he called out, "the tree is breaking. Hold on!"

He worked the paddle in a series of quick circular motions knowing the tree was splitting apart. Just as he was under the tree, it split in the middle and began a slow fall into the water, but the kayak moved fast enough that Martin just got past the thick and knobby old tree before it fell heavily into the creek. It sounded almost like the big hemlock was groaning as it split apart, and there was one last snap of the wood that was loud as thunder.

"Oh, my friend, Myra," Martin said, breathlessly "we just barely made it! That could have been the end for both of us."

The big hemlock had broken in such a way that it left a space of about ten feet between the two sides of the trunk that now sat in the water. Seeing this, Martin knew that when he returned from his trip to Glacier Pond that there would be enough space left by the fallen tree in the water to get home.

Home! The word seemed so dear to him now. He felt bad for the old hemlock because he knew it had just died right before his eyes, but he couldn't think too much about it because the long, straight stretch of Bender Creek still lay before him.

As he paddled onward his arms and legs felt numb. He could feel that his left hand was bleeding inside of his glove and his right hand felt raw too, but he knew he couldn't let go of the paddle. This was a deep pain like he'd never felt in his young life.

He clenched his teeth and closed his eyes, and, for some reason, at that moment he saw himself as a small orphan child back at Father Horrigan's Home for Boys.

He remembered at that moment what real suffering he'd felt when he was an orphan alone and unclaimed by anyone. He could feel tears form in his eyes. But just as quickly he could see in his mind's eye the faces of Papa Cider and Nonie just as they looked at him the first day they brought him home and the way they still looked at him every day since. The sight of them, the thought of them, gave him strength.

He looked ahead and could now see in the distance a large pool of smooth glimmering water beyond the last of the white rapids—it was Glacier Pond! Now he only had to make it through the last of the rapids, but these were the hardest and swiftest of all.

Once again, he closed his eyes and began to call out loud: "Dig...pull...pull..." Soon he lost his breath and could say nothing. His head became light, and he was afraid he might pass out completely, but he couldn't let up for even a second because the rapid waters would drive him downstream, and take him away from the Glacier Pond's still waters that would be a place of rest after his long journey.

He took a deep breath, closed his eyes, and kept plunging the paddle blades into the water with short, even, de-termined strokes. Then it happened! His paddling became suddenly easy. He opened his eyes and raised his head and saw that he was on a still, sunlit pond. He looked down at the water and could see to the bottom, twenty feet below, where quartz, copper, and other crystals glimmered on the sandy bottom—he had reached Glacier Pond, at last!

He took off his gloves and looked at his shaking hands. His right hand was sore and bleeding just a little, but the left hand was nearly covered with blood. He dipped his hands into the clean, pure waters and then wrapped a towel around the left one until it stung no more.

He removed the towel and took a long look at his left hand again. Old scar tissue was broken on it, and it felt less stiff, but it was still bleeding. He knew at that moment he could no longer put off the memory that he had for a long time been trying to forget. He was still breathing hard and feeling pain all over his body. He reached inside his t-shirt and felt for the scar on his chest to see if he was bleeding there too. It was at that second that a memory came back to him, almost too clearly. He was too exhausted to hold it back. It unfolded in his mind as plainly and clearly as any dream. It was clearer really, as he relived the scene as it happened many years earlier:

He saw himself as a small boy inside a dimly lit hospital room. He recalled a priest, Father Horrigan, coming into the room along with a man in a heavy winter overcoat. The man in the overcoat was taking notes.

A nurse stayed close to him in his bed where he lay with his left hand and arm wrapped in bandages; his bare chest burned despite the cooling lotion the nurse had put on it.

He heard the first words spoken by Father Horrigan: "You were a brave boy to run back into that house, Martin....but you couldn't save her. The fire and smoke were too much. You couldn't save your mother. But you tried, didn't you? You did what you could."

He saw Father Horrigan's head drop. He knew his mother was gone. The thick notebook of the man taking notes closed with a thud. Martin knew he was an orphan now as the men slowly walked out of the room.

The nurse softly touched his head, and he turned his face to hers: "But what happened to the big dark bird?"

The nurse moved closer, and he noticed her shining dark hair: "What bird, honey?"

"The one that saved me. He carried me away from the fire."

"That wasn't a bird, honey. It was a fireman."

"No," Martin said, his eyes beginning to close, "I thought I saw a bird."

"A fireman," Martin now said to himself as all was quiet around him except for the breeze moving the trees. What he remembered were dark wings enfolding him, but maybe it was the fireman's large coat. He remembered the large crest on the bird's head, but maybe it was a helmet. "I wonder where he is now... but I was sure I saw a bird! Then again, I was just a little boy, and my mother was gone."

He then said what he often said to himself: "I'm not an orphan anymore." Myra, hearing the sudden quiet, was trying to crawl out of her box, so Martin lifted her up and brought her close to his face: "We made it, Myra. How about a swim?"

"Swim," as always, was still the most delicious word for Myra. She began wiggling her legs in the air as she was lifted. Martin gently set her in the water, and she worked her little legs and began swimming in the sweet waters of Glacier Pond. Martin watched her for a while. He smiled and then lay back in the kayak, closed his eyes, and felt the sun on his face. It was a hard journey, but now it was worth it, worth every minute. He now understood something that had long been buried in the deep night of his memory and guarded by a large bird. He also knew something good was about to happen now that he'd reached Glacier Pond.

CHAPTER TWENTY-FOUR

Martin paddled the kayak to a large red granite rock that sloped into the water along the shore of Glacier Pond. He tied the kayak's front tether rope around the trunk of a small tree.

Myra had followed Martin in the water and when she reached the slab of granite rock, she clambered onto it and crawled up to where Martin was lying back and taking a long drink from his canteen.

Myra, settled next to Martin and extended her back legs and clawed feet so she could feel the sun's warmth on them. "Nice," she said. "This place is...friendly."

"Well, I hope it's friendly, Myra. We've come a long, long way. Just think of it, Myra—we made it all the way up Bender Creek!"

"You sure did," a voice called out. It was Cheevis whose head had just popped out of the water near the rock where Martin and Myra were sitting.

Cheevis climbed up the rock, shook himself as usual, and got water all over Martin and Myra.

"Making it up Bender Creek—wow, Kid. And now you're at Glacier Pond where the *real* miracles start to happen."

Just as he said that there was the sound of fluttering wings as Florelle landed on the rock and startled Myra who quickly pulled her head into her shell.

A few loose white feathers floated in the air and one landed on Cheevis' wet little nose, and he promptly sneezed, but the feather stayed on his nose so he shook his head from side to side and let out a few more sneezes until the feather drifted away.

"Well, Florelle," Cheevis said once he had stopped sneezing, "I see you *finally* made it here. Of course, you did it the easy way using your wings. While I was swimming up against this wicked current, I was just thinking, gee it sure must be nice to take it easy and just flap your wings and *fly* the whole way."

Cheevis knew very well that this would ruffle Florelle's feathers a little, so he looked over her way with his mischievous, beady, little dark eyes as he waited for her reaction.

"Outrageous!" Florelle said, sputtering mad. "Flying is not so easy you...you slippery little carnivore! I'll have you know, I was in great danger all the way up the creek. There can be tricky winds above a river, you know."

"All right, all right, Florelle, I was just kidding. Calm down now. I guess that flying is probably—well—not as easy as it looks."

Florelle had not finished. "One down-draft and I could have fallen into the rapids. I could have *crashed.* Why, what would the world have been like without sunny Florelle and my lovely black-tipped wings? Such sweetness gone, gone forever from the world."

Myra couldn't help letting out a little squeaking laugh and Martin smiled at Florelle.

"All right, all right, Florelle. You're just fine. Nothing bad happened to you, and we're just all really glad you made it," Martin said.

"Yes, come on, Florelle," Cheevis added, "we don't have time for any of your goose-fits. The big deer, the man himself, should be coming by any minute now, so let's all get ready."

"The pie-pie-pie-hole deer?" Myra asked. She looked around at the others for approval because the name was very hard for her to say.

"Close enough, my little turtle friend," Cheevis said.

"So do you know when he'll be coming?' Martin asked.

"Any minute now, Kid. Just look across the pond to where those twin pines are—see the two pines joined at the trunk? The Piebald comes out of the woods from behind there every day to take a look at his pond. This is really *his* place and all of the other animals want it that way. So just look over there, and any minute he should come out."

Martin looked down at Myra and was glad he would be sharing this moment with her: "Are you ready, Myra? This is what we came for."

There was an unusual quiet. Even Cheevis and Florelle went completely quiet. A snow goose, an otter, a young boy, and a turtle all sat side-by-side in perfect silence looking across the still water of Glacier Pond.

And then it happened, and when it did, it seemed like a dream to Martin.

Small fir trees and ferns moved behind the twin pines.

Very slowly and quietly the Piebald Deer stepped out of the dark woods and into the full light on the shore of Glacier Pond. His size nearly took Martin's breath away. He seemed tall as a horse. He had a wide rack of antlers. His coat was a very light tan with brown and white splashes and broad dark stripes like strokes painted by an artist's large brush, just as Nonie had described it. He was exceptional, unlike any other deer Martin or anyone else normally would see.

The Piebald looked across to where Martin and the others were seated on the rock far across the pond. He showed no fear. He came to the pond's edge and drank, raised his head, and looked again over toward Martin and his friends.

"Hello, sir," Martin said, not even knowing if the big deer could hear or understand him.

"He doesn't talk," Cheevis said in a hushed voice. "He doesn't *have* to talk."

"But he talked to me in a dream once. I know he did. It was before I was even adopted."

"Then you've been visited by him, Kid. He's like a prince in these mountains, and if he talked to you, you might be a prince too, but it may take awhile for you to know it."

"I know him," Myra said quietly as she stretched out her neck and watched the Piebald across the pond.

"Do you, Myra?" Martin asked softly. He was about to ask Myra where she'd met the Piebald Deer, but he kept quiet instead. He knew some things about Myra's life, but he also knew there were other things about her life he would never know. And maybe that was the way things should be, and that animals should have their own mysteries inside their own worlds, just beyond the reach of people, even the people who loved them.

The Piebald took one last look over the pond. During all the time he was present, everything grew quiet and still, and the waters of Glacier Pond had smoothed into glass.

He slowly turned away, stepped past the twin pines and into the darkness of the woods and the mountain meadows, ravines and streams and the twisted, wind-weathered mountain-top trees from where he'd come. As he passed through small spruce trees the branches snapped and bits of early-evening dew burst with little rainbow colors. At last Martin, Myra, Cheevis, and Florelle could hear only the fading sound of the deer's last steps.

Martin was still a little breathless. It had all happened so fast. After the exhausting journey up Bender's Creek, the sight of the Piebald, amazing as it was, was now over —and then he heard three words.

"Magnificent, isn't he?"

It was a voice, a girl's voice, and it was both soft and powerful, and it was coming from behind him.

All at once, Martin and his friends turned to see where the voice was coming from.

About twenty feet behind them they saw a girl about Martin's age walking toward them. She was tall and lanky, wearing faded blue jeans. She had a well-worn brown t-shirt that had the image of a small deer stitched in white thread near her shoulder. Her hair was so long it went past her waist and was brownish and sun-bleached golden blonde on the outer layers. With her long tanned arms and the pace of her walk, she looked quick and wild and alert in a way that Martin immediately liked. She must have spent a lot of her time in the woods and around water as he did.

Always polite, Martin awkwardly scrambled to his feet, and he could hear the girl giggle a little as he forced a nervous smile. As she came closer, Martin could see her eyes were blue-green and clear like the water in Glacier Pond. He could see that the round irises of her eyes were flecked with little splashes of gold.

The girl extended her arm to shake hands with Martin who tried to say something but was a little overwhelmed by the moment. She saw his hand had been bleeding, and she took a longer look into his eyes and smiled a little sadly. Martin had the strange feeling she understood him.

"My name is Cress," the girl said. "It's short for Cressida."

Martin felt her warm hand in his, and he struggled to say something but was still tongue-tied. He looked down and saw that Cheevis and Florelle were completely mum just as they always were when they were around any person other than Martin.

Myra took a different approach. She extended her neck and opened her mouth as if about to say something, and out came such a tiny "hello" that Martin was sure Cress couldn't hear it.

Cress bent down, brushed her hair back, and looked at Myra: "And hello to you there, little turtle. What's your name?"

Myra's mouth opened wide once again, but nothing but a little burp could be heard.

Cress and Martin both laughed, and it broke the ice enough that now Martin had regained his composure.

"She's Myra. I'm Martin. I live at Three Tamaracks over on Orenda Lake."

"And what about you two?" Cress said looking down at Cheevis and Florelle. Florelle turned away and pretended to be grooming her feathers.

"Oh, they won't say anything now," Martin said, "but maybe if you get to know them."

"Of course," Cress said cheerfully, "I hear creatures talk all the time."

This gratified Martin and the thought suddenly struck him: was Cress's presence the "wonderful thing" Cheevis and Florelle had said would happen when he came to Glacier Pond?

Cress folded her arms and looked suddenly serious: "Is this the first time you came to see the Piebald Deer?"

"Yep, and it was worth the trip. Have you seen him before?"

Cress nodded her head and her fine, sun-bleached eyebrows arched a little: "Well, sure! I see him a lot. I don't live far from here. Just across a few blueberry meadows and up a mountainside."

She tossed back her hair and looked across the Glacier Pond and then moved her face so close to Martin's that he gulped: "You mustn't tell people about this place, Martin. Do you hear me?" She said it in nearly a whisper.

"Sure," Martin said, a little taken aback, "but why?"

"Because it's for the animals. They don't have many places left that are completely their own. Bender Creek protects this place. It doesn't let many come through. You're one of the few, and I think I know why. You love these kinds of places, don't you? I can see it in you. Look at the friends you have here."

Martin was more and more fascinated with Cress, and he had the feeling he should say something before she headed home: "Um...Cress...I could probably row my way back up Bender Creek next week and maybe, just maybe..."

Cress smiled and seemed a little charmed by his stammering. "Maybe what, Martin?"

"Oh, maybe I could—um—visit you and we could talk and...."

"No," she said kindly enough, "I don't tell people exactly where my mother and I live. There are about fourteen paths back to our cottage. Maybe someday, Martin."

This wasn't quite what Martin wanted to hear, but he understood.

"Well, I have to be off, now. My mother will wonder what happened to me."

"Sure," Martin said, now sounding a little dejected.

Cress did a deft leap over a fallen log and reached into a duffle bag and pulled out some gauze and adhesive tape and a tube of ointment and walked back to where he was standing. Then, without a word, she carefully touched and lifted Martin's left hand and dabbed some ointment on it. She very gently placed a couple of gauze pads on the wounded scar tissue. She then quickly and expertly wrapped some pieces of adhesive tape over the gauze.

He started to thank her, but she just shook her head and smiled.

"You'll be back here. I know it, Martin. You love this place, and this place loves you. Just like all these creatures—Myra, and this lovely snow goose, and this handsome otter."

When Cheevis heard the words "handsome otter" his

eyes closed with pleasure as he always did when he received a compliment.

Then Cress did something that surprised everyone, especially Martin. She took a quick step forward and brought her face close to his and gave him a light little butterfly's kiss on the cheek.

Martin felt something like warm electricity going through his entire body.

With that, she ambled off, picked up a duffle bag, and followed a path into the woods, her long legs moving quickly as she stepped lightly and deftly over thick roots and rocks on the path. She turned and gave a last wave. "Goodbye, Martin. So long, all of you. Good-bye!"

Her rich voice echoed over the pond as she said these last words, and soon she was out of sight.

"Good...bye, Cress," Martin called, a little faintly.

"What a girl she was!" Florelle said in a cheery, honking voice.

Martin's cheek still tingled where Cress had left her kiss. It was all true: something wonderful had happened at Glacier Pond and the Piebald Deer was just part of it.

CHAPTER TWENTY-FIVE

The sun began sinking beneath the tall pines on the west side of Glacier Pond. Martin never wore a wristwatch, but like many people who live close to nature, he could guess what time it was by watching the sun. He knew he must start back to Orenda Lake before it became too late.

Now that he'd be heading downstream on Bender Creek, the rapids might help him to move along quickly, but he still had to be alert to rocks and other hazards in the water. He filled his canteen with the clear, cold water from the pond and carefully pulled on a leather glove over his bandaged hand.

Florelle and Cheevis sat quietly side-by-side on the large granite rock while Myra began to crawl her way toward the kayak and then stopped to wait for Martin who was gazing out at the pond.

Martin noticed that Cheevis and Florelle looked a little solemn, and he wasn't sure why.

"Well, you two," Martin said cheerfully, "Myra and I

better get going or Nonie will call the Orenda Lake rescue squad if I'm not home soon. How about if the both of you stop over to Three Tamaracks next week? Nonie will have some crackers for you, Florelle, and maybe a couple of sardines for you, Cheevis."

After a long pause, Cheevis spoke: "No, this is it, Kid," Cheevis said glumly.

Florelle simply hung her head.

"What do you mean 'This is it'? I don't understand."

Martin looked for a long time at his friends, the otter and snow goose he'd come to know so well.

"Well, we're not getting any younger," Cheevis began, "and we have things we have to do. Florelle wants to head north and find her home. Remember, Martin, she was blown off course when she was just a young goose."

Martin was stunned. He stepped closer to the two and squatted down so he could look them in the eyes.

"And me," Cheevis continued, "I'm thinking of exploring the Pike River. A lot of otters live there, they tell me. And after all, our work is done here."

"Wait a minute," Martin said with a little anger rising in his voice, "what do you mean your 'work is done'? Was that your plan all along, to get me to Glacier Pond and then leave me behind—for good?"

Now it was Florelle's turn to speak: "We can't tell you everything. But, yes, we wanted to get you here, and now your life will be changed."

"What she means," Cheevis continued, "is that we animals have our own secrets. We knew we had to get you here, but we can't tell you everything. We knew that once we got you here that your life would be changed forever, but you won't know how for many years maybe, but we were happy to help you. Let's leave it at that, Martin."

"Wow," Martin exclaimed, "this is the first time you ever called me by my name, Cheevis. Usually, you just call me 'Kid.'"

"But you're not a kid anymore, Martin. You paddled up a dangerous creek, and you've seen a place most people never see, and you even met Cress. Just think about all of that, Martin."

Martin was more sad than angry and his voice trembled: "But I'll *miss* you, don't you see?"

With that Cheevis and Florelle both entered the water of the pond. The late afternoon sun had left an orange-gold tint on the water. As they swam away side-by-side, Cheevis and Florelle both looked like they were creatures painted on an old canvas with the slightest glaze of the sun's gold leaf.

Florelle began honking in a way that made her sound like she was crying, maybe knowing she would never see Martin or Myra—or even Cheevis—again.

Cheevis called back to Martin, "You'll always have Myra."

Martin reached for Myra and lifted her onto his lap.

"There they go, Myra. We'll sure miss them, won't we?"

By now Florelle and Cheevis were far out into the pond, and it looked like they were bickering at each other, but maybe it was not that.

"I'm sure glad I still have you with me, Myra."

Myra, happy on Martin's lap, stretched her neck and looked up toward his face, and said one word: "Always."

"You know, for a little turtle who doesn't talk all that much, you have a way of finding the right words."

With that, he lifted her up and began to carry her toward the kayak. He then stopped and held her high over his head and looked up at her.

"You turtles live for a long time. Maybe, just maybe, we'll live for a long time together. And I promise I'll come up to see you every summer."

Myra then said the word again: "Always."

"So, let's get on our way, Myra. It's time to head back. Just you and me, right?"

"Right," the little Painted Turtle said. At that moment, a snow goose flew high over Glacier Pond. Martin knew it was Florelle finally beginning the search for her true home. Life was changing.

PART TWO

CHAPTER TWENTY-SIX

Years passed. Martin was now twenty-two years of age and stood over six feet tall. His hair was dark brown and wavier than when he was a boy. He stared out the screen door and watched cars noisily splash down the street on this rainy day. It had been only two weeks since he'd graduated from college and received his degree in biology, but he wasn't thinking about that now.

Graduation might have been the beginning of a happy summer, but Martin's shoulders sagged as he looked out the door and rubbed his bloodshot eyes. He had not even begun packing for the annual summer trip to Orenda Lake and "Three Tamaracks." This year was different.

Papa Cider was very sick, and the house was quiet except for the sound of birds in the dripping rhododendron and lilac bushes outside the house. Everything in the house had come to a standstill. A shadow had fallen over the wall photos of Papa Cider, Martin, and Nonie posing before trees, mountainsides or at the beach, or on the porch at their beloved camp. In each framed photo on the tables or bookshelves, the sun of those past summers seemed to have gone behind dark clouds.

A weak voice called from a small downstairs bedroom. Martin took a deep breath, straightened his shoulders, and turned toward the little lighted room where Papa Cider lay: "I'm coming, Papa. I'll be right there."

Papa Cider was sitting up in the bed; several pillows propped him up. He was thinner now and his cheeks were hollow, but when he saw Martin, his bushy eyebrows raised and he managed a smile: "Well, there's my boy. And a college graduate, no less!"

"You look better, Papa Cider. Could I get you a cup of tea or something?"

"No, no thanks, Martin. I'm enjoying the sound of those gold finches and chickadees outside, and I think I heard a phoebe out there too. They sound happy. Birds love a good warm rain."

Papa paused, and he seemed to lose his breath for a second: "Is Nonie still out?"

"Grocery shopping," Martin said, "and then a stop at the drug store and the post office."

"Good. I'm glad she finally took a break. You know, she's exhausting herself. I'm more concerned about her than me."

"She's just worried about you, Papa. We both want you to get well."

"Well, I guess so, but...just look at you! Our son, the college graduate! And now you're planning to go to graduate school and major in, in—what was that funny word?"

"Herpetology, Papa. It means I'll be studying reptiles. You know how much I've always been interested in turtles. I'd like to write books about turtles, maybe soon."

Papa laughed softly. "Well, you sure know an awful lot about turtles after all your years with Myra and a talking turtle at that! Not that I ever heard her speak. But there was always some magic between you and that smiley little turtle."

They both grew silent. The name "Myra" was a reminder of Three Tamaracks and Orenda Lake and the surrounding mountains. They seemed far away now.

"Martin, since Nonie's gone right now, I want to ask you for a couple of big favors. First of all, if I miss this trip."

"Oh, you'll make the trip, Papa Cider. I know you will!"

"Well...maybe so," Papa Cider said doubtfully, "but if I *can't*, I want you to promise me that you and Nonie make it up there this year, and I want the two of you to *always* go up. Are you hearing me on that, Martin? The other thing is, please don't let Nonie worry too much." He chuckled a little. "Why that good woman worries about me, worries about you, worries about everything. She can worry looking forward and she can worry in reverse and sideways too."

They both laughed for a moment.

"And I have one more thing I want you to do before Nonie comes back."

"Sure. Anything, Papa Cider."

"That canoe paddle that's been set above the fireplace all these years? I want you to go get it and bring it in here."

Martin was a little puzzled at this request, but he left the room and came back with the paddle.

Papa Cider reached up and took the paddle from Martin and put it across his lap as he sat up in the bed. He ran his hands along the smooth wood.

"Always loved the feel of a good custom-made paddle.

Many, many years ago my father made this down in his basement workshop. I can still smell those pine wood-shavings left on the floor. Look at that small circle he etched up near the top. When he gave it to me he said 'Son, someday you'll have a long journey to take and this is the paddle you'll want to use.'"

"It's sure a beauty, Papa."

"Well, it's yours, Martin. I've been waiting for the right time to give it to you and now's as good a time as any. You have a long journey in front of you and whenever it gets difficult just hold onto this for a while."

"I've always had my eye on it all those years it was sitting above the fireplace."

"One more thing, Martin. Just for a while I want to keep it here next to my bed. I want to be able to hold onto it in the days ahead. You see, I've had some pretty wild dreams lately. I keep dreaming of rivers and lakes—lakes with no names—all this bright water up ahead of me."

"That's the best of dreams, Papa Cider."

"Anyway, my son, that bright water looks an awful lot like Orenda Lake after the morning fog lifts and the sun hits the water for the first time."

Martin kept quiet. He knew there was more Papa Cider wanted to tell him before Nonie came home.

"You see," Papa continued, "I may be heading on my own journey soon. I don't mean that in a sad way at all. I mean I'm heading to some country. No name for it, I guess, just a place where I'll have a river to cross and woods to walk in. And maybe I'll see some firelight in the woods one night, and I'll hear some familiar voices calling to me, and I'll follow a path I can barely see and..."

"Oh, Papa," Martin said now, his voice very soft, and

unsteady, "you and Nonie have meant so much to me. Just look what you've done for me."

"Not as much as what you did for us, Martin. I should be thanking you."

With that Papa Cider weakly raised one hand. He was too tired to speak anymore. He closed his eyes and drifted off to sleep—and dreams of rivers and lakes and a fire in the woods.

"Sweet dreams, Papa." Martin kissed him on the forehead and then turned off the lamp next to Papa's bed. At the same moment, Nonie's car came into the driveway. The rain stopped and all was silent.

CHAPTER TWENTY-SEVEN

It would be a long quiet ride in the car up to Orenda Lake for Martin and Nonie now that Papa Cider was no longer with them. Martin kept a promise to Papa Cider that he and Nonie would continue to go up to Three Tamaracks each summer. As sad as they felt, once they approached the narrow dirt road that led to the camp, they knew they had made the right decision. Their family camp and Orenda Lake was a sacred place for Papa Cider, and they'd always feel his presence long after he quietly passed away. Soon they'd be hearing that sweet music when strong winds came across the lake and made the shaken tamaracks sing.

When Martin and Nonie arrived at Three Tamaracks, they quickly got to work on the usual first-day chores. Martin took the plywood boards off the windows and Nonie swept out the cottage and hung small carpets on an outside clothesline.

The two of them worked quietly. They were happy to be busy. Nonie usually sang or whistled when she worked, but this year she was quiet as she moved on to the kitchen and emptied the dishes from the cupboard and began to clean the shelves.

They both could feel the absence of Papa Cider everywhere they looked. They missed him and knew Three Tamaracks would not be the same without him.

Nonie picked up one of Papa's old caps that said, "Smoke Lake." She looked down at it for a second. "Cyrus liked this old cap for some reason. Must have left it up here last summer." She set the cap down again and bit her lip and shook her head.

Martin began gathering up old magazines left on a side-table next to the frayed stuffed chair that Papa Cider used to sit in. The magazines had bookmarks placed in them wherever Papa had found something he thought was worth returning to read again. There were articles with titles like "Ten Uses for Linseed Oil You Never Thought Of," or "Eggs: the Miracle Protein," or "The Pickle and Sauerkraut Diet Method."

Martin had gathered the magazines with the idea of throwing them away, but now he wasn't sure. He simply placed them in a box to be taken home at the end of the vacation.

Nonie took a seat in the rattan chair near the fireplace where she always sat opposite Papa Cider. Martin leaned down beside her chair: "Are you all right, Nonie?"

Nonie shook her head: "It will take time, Martin. That's all I can say. It will take time."

"I know," Martin said and then he rose to his feet, and then said cheerfully, "But we'll be all right, won't we Nonie? That's the way he would have wanted it, right?"

"You're right about that, Martin. He wouldn't want us

moping around."

Martin yawned and stretched his long arms. "Well, I think I'll head down to the beach. I think Myra might be coming by soon, and I want to give her a proper greeting. At least I *hope* she'll be coming by soon. She's still a wild creature and with the tough winters up here you never know if she's made it through."

"Oh, I have a feeling Myra will be here," Nonie said, smiling to herself. "Every year I see that little turtle, and I can't help but feel happy."

Over the years that Martin had been growing up, Myra had continued to visit the camp every day in the summer. She no longer lived in the Big Marsh. She had moved to a tiny, swampy little bay just down the lake from Three Tamaracks. The place was called Feaster Cove and it was too narrow or shallow for boats to enter, so Myra and her neighbors—frogs, beavers, other turtles, some ducks—were left in peace. Myra also had a short swim to get to Three Tamaracks each day.

Because she had spent so many summers with Martin, and always listened to him closely when he talked, she had become better with words over the years. Myra now could often speak in complete sentences. She was very proud of that. She only spoke when she thought it was necessary, and she still spoke only to Martin. She probably had her own way of speaking to turtles and other animals too, but that was another mystery that Martin left alone.

Martin sat in the same old rickety and weathered Adirondack chair on the beach as he awaited the first sight of Myra since the previous summer. Before long he saw the top of a black shell moving slowly toward the beach. Myra came out of the water, her shell wet and gleaming. She extended her neck and took a long look as she scanned the beach. When she spotted Martin her legs and flipper feet began clawing forward as quickly as she could make them move. Soon, as she approached, Martin could see the little smile on her face. She was now in her late-teen years and her red markings and yellow neck-stripes were more vivid than ever.

"Hello, Myra, my dear friend," Martin said bending down as she moved closer to his chair.

"Hello, Martin, my dear friend," the little voice called back.

Martin giggled to himself, hearing again how she often mimicked what he said and how carefully she took in every word he spoke.

"Oh, I'm so glad to see you, Myra. Seeing you makes me feel like it's truly summer again. Feels like home."

"Well, you *are* home!" she said, very happily. "Home is where Martin and Myra are, and right now they're—um, *we're*—right here on this beach and...." Myra lost her train of thought. It had been only a couple of years since she started stitching together full sentences, and she got a little messed up in the middle sometimes.

"Yep, Myra, another summer together."

Myra stretched her neck and blinked up at him as he sat in the chair: "May I?"

"Of course, Myra. Let's bring you up here on my lap. I'll fold this towel up and you'll be warm and cozy."

Once she was up on his lap, she turned her head upward to get a full look at his face as they talked: "And so, how are Nonie and Papa Cider?" she asked.

"Well, Nonie's here, and she's just fine. Papa Cider...well, he's gone, I'm sorry to say."

Myra blinked her eyes: "Where has he gone to?"

"That's hard to answer, Myra. He passed away just a couple of weeks ago."

Myra was not quite understanding what Martin was talking about: "Are *you* passing away?"

"I hope not, "Martin laughed. "No, Myra. You and I are not passing away anytime soon, at least I hope not. I hope we have a lot of years together."

Myra looked at him earnestly, "Will you tell me when you're going to pass away? I might want to come along...and where was it again? The ducks pass away to somewhere every fall and I'm just wondering...."

"Myra, Myra. Let's just not talk about passing away, okay? I'm not sure you're *getting* those words, not right now anyway. For now, it's just important that you and me are together, right? We'll have plenty of summers ahead of us."

"And we'll swim!" Myra said with delight.

"You bet we'll swim, Myra. Let's take a swim this afternoon."

After a few minutes on the warm towel on Martin's lap, Myra grew so comfortable that she extended her back legs to feel the sun's warmth on them and she closed her eyes and pulled her head into her shell a little ways. Martin said "aww" when he heard a tiny little snoring sound coming from Myra. He knew he couldn't move for a while, so he started thinking about his plan for the next day.

He looked out at the lake and could see how the water level had dropped during the recent drought. His little sandy beach in the cove on Three Tamaracks point was larger than ever because the water level in the lake had gone down. He looked up at the dry leaves in the trees and hoped there would not be a wildfire in the offing. Everything seemed to be dry and drooping, and it added to the sadness of Papa Cider's death.

Still, he had one driving desire that had been with him for a long while. He wanted to make a return to Glacier Pond. It was ten years since his only trip up Bender Creek. He wasn't completely sure of why he wanted to return. Surely the Piebald Deer was now gone. Then he thought of Cress. It seemed impossible that she would still be there if he went back, but he still wondered if he could find her. He had never quite forgotten her.

He decided that he would take the kayak again this time. He knew that with the drought, Bender Creek would have a lower water level and the rapids would not be as difficult. He'd leave Myra behind just for this trip.

As soon as he thought about all of this, he wondered if it were just an attempt to re-live a part of his past that would never come back. Should he even bother? It felt as if his boyhood was long gone, never to be found again.

At that moment, a crow flew overhead. Martin swore that whatever direction the crow flew would help determine if he would take the kayak trip or not. He'd learned the wisdom of crows over the years and how they always fly in the right direction. He shaded his eyes and watched the crow fly directly south, toward Bender Creek and Glacier Pond: "That's it then," he said, "tomorrow I'll go back to Glacier Pond."

CHAPTER TWENTY-EIGHT

As Martin paddled up Bender Creek in his kayak, he could not believe how much it had changed. The water level was so low in many places that his kayak scraped the sand and small stones on the creek's bottom. Gone were the fearsome rapids of earlier years. Now the current was strong only in a few places but sluggish and slow in most stretches of the creek.

The trees along the bank of the creek looked parched with some leaves turning papery and brown even though it was only early summer. Now there were spindly, rotting trees leaning, broken and bare, in many places along the banks of the creek. Years of thunderstorms, hard winters, and summer drought had brought them down.

Because he was now a young man, Martin was bigger and stronger, so he made his way up Bender Creek fairly quickly as he worked the kayak paddle vigorously. Sooner than he thought, he was entering the still waters of Glacier Pond. Immediately he smelled a strong odor, and he knew that it was from the stagnant waters of the pond where a large field of green algae had formed on the surface.

"You poor pond," he said. "You're all tied up. Not much joy left in you."

He then looked up at the skies and made a wish that rain might come and refresh Glacier Pond and Bender Creek and bring back rippling, clear and deep waters.

He steered his kayak over to the big slab of granite that sloped into the water. It was the same place he had parked his wooden kayak ten years earlier, but now the slab of rock was bigger because the water level of Glacier Pond had gone down in the drought.

Once out of his kayak, he looked across the pond to the space near the twin pines where once the Piebald Deer had stood so majestically. The trail that the Piebald had followed had now been widened. Martin could see that someone had taken a chain saw and cut away trees and shrubs to make a wider trail. "It's been found," Martin said to himself, "and it's never going to be the same."

He sat down on the big red rock and pulled a candy bar out of his backpack. As he ate, memories filled his mind. He could picture Cheevis swimming on his back, always the joker. He laughed remembering how Cheevis had stumbled on the word "platypus."

He also remembered graceful and frustrated Florelle and how she and Cheevis annoyed each other but remained strangely devoted to their friendship. Thinking back, Martin was most amazed to remember how they had connived to get him to Glacier Pond on the very day that he saw the Piebald Deer and that mysterious girl—Cress. What ever had happened to Cress? She had appeared on a day that seemed magical as he looked back on it. But now it seemed that Glacier Pond was suffering, so he wondered if it had any magic left in it.

He sat still on the rock and took in the sights. Mallards passed low above the pond's waters, but even they refused to land on a pond so choked by algae. He shook his head. He knew it was silly to think he'd ever see Cress again.

It was then that he heard soft footsteps behind him and felt a shadow fall over him. He quickly looked up and saw the face of a young woman. He was startled and jumped to his feet: "Whoa! Excuse me...um...who are you?"

But before the young woman could say anything he looked into her eyes and could see splashes of gold in her irises. He saw the long brown hair that reached her waist: "Cress?"

She smiled at him. It was a radiant smile. "You remember me, Martin?"

He stuttered for a second in surprise: "Why, why...sure I r-remember you. In fact, I've thought about you for...." He stopped, not sure if he wanted to tell her that right now.

"Martin, I always thought you'd come back sooner. How long ago was it?"

"Ten years." Martin blurted it out a little too firmly, and he heard Cress giggle a little.

"And you never came back again that summer," Cress said. Her smile was so warm that it relaxed Martin—at least a little.

"No, I barely made it up Bender Creek the first time."

"But I told you we'd meet again," Cress said brightly. "I always think that when two people are meant to meet...." This time it was she who blushed as if she knew she'd said too much. "Not that we were exactly *meant* to meet."

"But then, well, maybe we *were* meant to meet again, Cress. You were right when you said it the first time here at Glacier Pond." Martin surprised himself by saying this. Everything was happening so fast that his head was spinning. How could they feel so familiar with each other after ten years apart?

Cress was at ease and still smiling. She always had a graceful way of tossing her long hair, and Martin was so fascinated to see her as a tall, grown woman that he was having a hard time keeping up with the conversation.

"So, what's happened to you over the years, Martin?"

"Well, I just got my college degree. It's in biology."

"Very appropriate" Cress nodded. "You were surrounded by all these wild little creatures the day I saw you."

"Yep. I'm going on to graduate school now to study herpetology. That means—"

"I *know* what it means, Martin. It's the study of reptiles. For me, it's birds. I'm working now at a rehabilitation center for birds. We take in injured birds, mostly raptors like hawks and eagles and falcons. Some have been hit by cars or even shot. I try to fix what's wrong with them. But some have to stay because they're too injured to return to the wild. So, Martin, are you going to be a professor, or a teacher, or what?"

"Something like that. I want to study and write books— about turtles mainly. You might remember when I brought a turtle with me last time."

"Myra!" Cress said.

"That's her name."

"Is she still...?"

"Alive? You bet. She's back at the camp right now. Turtles can live for many years, you know. She's my good friend. Most people wouldn't understand that."

"Oh, I understand completely," Cress said.

She then tipped her head back and looked up into the skies. "You know, I've been hoping for rain. This pond is my favorite place in the world. I just hope those rain clouds stop over here. Everything is thirsty."

Martin was finding courage in all this talk. He was still amazed at Cress's ability to make him feel so relaxed. He'd spent his college years studying hard and never had a true girlfriend, but he felt it was now time to say something that was on his mind from the second he saw Cress just a few moments earlier.

He cleared his throat, and when he spoke, he could hear a slightly embarrassing shrillness in his voice: "Cress... um, there's a dance down at the West Scotus Town Hall Saturday night. I guess it's the kind of music with fiddles and a banjo and...you know, sort of *that* kind of music. And I was just wondering...and if you can't do it, just tell me and I'll...."

"I'd love to go, Martin. And you know what? I hope there are a few slow dances."

Martin was so surprised at her quick answer that he was tongue-tied again: "Well that's...that's just fine. Where should I pick you up? Well, not *pick you up*, but you know...."

"Oh, Martin," Cress said, laughing again, "you *are* a very dear man. Funny too."

With that, she surprised him again by hugging him. Slowly he put his arms around her and it seemed as if they couldn't let go. They both closed their eyes for a moment as if they were old friends who had just rediscovered each other after a few years, even though they'd spent so little time together. But now time had vanished, and they simply wanted to hold each other.

Once they let go, they both laughed a little nervously and looked down at the ground.

"So, I'll come up here to get you at about, let's say, five-thirty on Saturday?"

Cress smiled at him and tilted her head: "No need to work so hard and row all the way up Bender Creek, Martin. I know every path along the creek. There's one that goes all the way to the landing where the creek meets Orenda Lake. I'll be out there waiting for you. Maybe I should bring my fiddle."

They both laughed.

"All right," Martin said. "I'll come to meet you in my Papa's Guide Boat. In the meantime, I guess I better practice my dancing."

With that, he was surprised again as he saw Cress's face come towards him. She gave him the same light little butterfly's kiss on the cheekbone she had given him ten years ago. He again felt as he did ten years earlier, something electric went through all his limbs, and then he felt happily free and unburdened in a way he hadn't for a while.

Cress was off as quickly as she came. She still seemed like the sprightly, athletic girl from the "Back Ponds" area as she stepped and hopped over roots and rocks with the ease of a dancer. She gave that same quick little wave from a distance.

"Oh, Papa Cider," Martin said, as if to the sky itself, "you'd really like this girl."

Then a cold raindrop fell on his head, and then another. Then hundreds tapped the surface of Glacier Pond. Martin had never been so happy to see rain fall. All the trees and bushes drank thirstily. Soon the slow current would begin moving in Glacier Pond and the old stagnant water would be pushed out. The pond would find its movement, its joy again. That is, if you believe ponds have their own joyful days.

CHAPTER TWENTY-NINE

A year later Martin and Cress were married lakeside on the beach at Three Tamaracks. Cress wore a long silky white dress and a garland of wildflowers on her head.

A minister, Reverend Leland Butterby, drove up from Mohican Hollow to perform the ceremony. He stood behind a long, white-clothed table and delivered the wedding vows. At one point a busy hummingbird flew in quick, jerky circles around his head.

Nonie wept, as some people do at weddings, but she heartily approved of Cress and knew she was a fine match for Martin.

A few of Cress's and Martin's friends also wept. Some of the guests were people who'd grown up with Martin or Cress. Some of Cress's friends who worked with her at the bird rehabilitation center were present. There were also Martin's friends, many of whom were finishing their studies in various areas involving the science of plants, birds, or rocks or conservation. Most of the young people at the wedding seemed to have some career planned that had to do with forests and creatures although there was one genial bald chemist and one plumber who was writing a novel.

Cress took the time to fashion a tiny garland of daisy petals that she placed on Myra's head.

For most of the ceremony and recital of wedding vows, Myra plodded her way in circles around the sandy beach. From time to time, she'd stop and extend her long neck to look up at one of the wedding guests. Because Cress and Martin's friends were all animal lovers, they'd bend down and smile at the turtle they'd heard so much about, but probably none suspected that she talked. She saved her talking for Martin, but Cress was the one other person who could hear her talk.

Later, inside the cabin, Martin's chosen "best man" lifted a glass of champagne and offered a toast to the newly married couple: "To two grand people who found each other out in these wild Adirondack woods. May you always be happy and live in places as wild and lovely as Orenda Lake."

At that point, leaning on her cane, Nonie added her piece to the toast: "And how many of us can ever say we went to a wedding where a turtle served as a flower girl?"

Everyone laughed. The wedding cake was cut and slices on small plates were passed around. Myra was given a special serving of fresh fruits on a dessert plate, and she happily tugged away at the fruit pieces while others ate cake and sipped drinks.

As was often his way, Martin sat back quietly and observed the cheerful room. He watched Nonie moving slowly with her cane, and he wondered how many more years she could make it up to the lake. He watched how gracefully Cress found her way around the room, moving from guest to guest. In her white dress and with the garland still on her head, she looked to him like the paintings of Guinevere in his old childhood books about King Arthur.

He took a deep breath and felt like the luckiest man in the world at that moment. He closed his eyes trying to hold every detail of the night in his memory so he would never forget it.

At the same time, he was old enough to know he couldn't hold on to the moment as tightly as he wished. Other days would come, but he'd still try to remember every detail: the crackling fire, the friends who'd come together in honor of him and Cress; Nonie, who, he thought, must be remembering the summer when she married Papa Cider.

Martin also wanted to remember the turtle who was with him during the loneliest time in his boyhood and was with him still. But he also knew that things change even as he wished he could hold this picture forever.

CHAPTER THIRTY

The two of them sat quietly next to each other as the sun went down. They were up on the balcony porch of the cottage at Three Tamaracks. Martin rocked back on his weathered wicker chair, and Cress put aside her magazine. They could see the lake had reached a perfect stillness. As the last of dusk fell a few boats on the lake puttered and hummed their way back to their distant cottages where the dock lights were just coming on.

Martin reached over and took Cress's hand. It was a perfect moment. They watched where fish nosed up to the glassy surface of the lake and left circles in the water. A long, deep shadow had scaled Patchen Mountain and only the pines on the very top of the peak were still lit from the last sunset fire cast by the dropping sun. A single loon let out a piercing call, waited, only to hear only its own voice bouncing off the mountain and calling back.

Cress squeezed Martin's hand: "So I guess this is the anniversary we spend alone, huh?"

They both chuckled.

"Yeah, but this is fine, Cress. Maybe a little lonelier here with Nonie staying home this year."

Cress lifted her hand and put it on Martin's shoulder: "It's been five years now. Any regrets? And you better not say 'yes' there, Turtle Guy."

"Are you kidding?' Martin laughed. "It's been an amazing five years. I'm sure glad I found myself a wild girl right out of the Back Ponds country. Wild like one of your birds, right? And how do you feel about being married to a guy who talks with a turtle? Weird, huh?"

"Well, I guess we'll be weird together because I could always understand what birds were saying. So yeah, I guess I'll always be that wild 'Back Ponds' girl." Cress paused for a second. "I sure do miss seeing Nonie here."

"Me too," Martin said. "But she insisted. That walker she has makes it hard to get around here now, and it's never been quite the same up here since Papa Cider passed away."

"I'm glad that some things *don't* change," Cress said firmly. "We still have Myra coming by to visit us every day. I hope that goes on for a long time."

Martin thought about that and said nothing.

"I know turtles live a long time, but how long, Martin?"

"Sometimes as long as a human—sometimes longer. You know, she said she'll always remember how kind she and Papa were to her. She remembers pretty much everything. Never speaks to anyone else but me."

"Hey, I've heard her speak quite a few times! But, yeah, she speaks mostly to you. What a turtle!" Martin could see that the gold flecks in Cress's irises were lit up like small flames by the little bit of lamplight on the porch. "There's something magic about Myra, isn't there? She's like a little painted goddess stepping out of the water each day." Cress said it almost breathlessly.

"You know, Cress, when she came up on the beach here as a baby so many years ago and we took her in, I watched as her shell mended, and I was so happy I could help her. Funny thing is, I think she was the one who healed me even more. I felt like the loneliest kid in the world back then. All those years in the Boys' Home almost broke me, and then there was that fire when I was a kid and losing my mother. But then Nonie and Papa came into my life. And then along came this little turtle."

Martin dropped his head and wiped a tear from his cheek and took a deep breath of the cool mountain air.

"Martin, are you all right? I know you must miss Papa Cider, and it's lonelier without Nonie here this year, but...."

"It's not just that, Cress. It's just that I look around this lake and camp and everywhere I see a memory. How can I ever say goodbye?"

"Goodbye? To Three Tamaracks...and Orenda Lake? What are you talking about? We're *always* coming up here, right?"

Martin took another deep breath. "Cress, do you remember when I told you I had an interview at the college when those three people flew in from California?"

"Yes, but you never talked about it much after that."

"Well, I had a lot to think about. You see, they offered me a job, a job that I never would have allowed myself to even dream about."

"That sounds wonderful!"

"It is. They're starting a center for the study of turtles

in San Francisco—sea turtles, land turtles, all turtles. And it will have exhibits where the people can see the turtles up close. Turns out they want me to be the director. I guess they'd read a lot of the articles and studies of turtles I've written and, well, they think I'm the guy for the job."

"That's all good, Martin. Right? And in San Francisco! How exciting is that?"

"Well, that's the problem.? We'll have to move to the West Coast."

Now it hit Cress. "Oh...oh, I see. But we're still coming up here every summer...right? Right?"

"I won't have summers off any more like I did when I was teaching."

"But there must be a way we could come back here. We could rent it out for a few weeks in the summer."

Martin shook his head. "I promised Papa Cider that I'd always take care of this place, but I can't if we're out in San Francisco. I won't be able to come up in the winter and check in on the place or stop in after a big storm hits. And then there's..." He couldn't quite say it.

"Myra! We can't take Myra? Is that what you're saying, Martin?"

"This lake is her home, Cress. I'm not going to haul her out to California and put her in an aquarium for the rest of her life. It wouldn't be fair."

Cress nodded sadly. Orenda Lake and its surrounding areas once were her home too, and still were in the summertime. She couldn't find an argument for taking Myra away from there.

"I'm not sure what I'll tell her yet. I say goodbye to her every year. But this will be the last time. I'll need time with her alone tomorrow. I hope I can say it in a way she understands."

"You will, Martin," Cress said as she lightly tapped her index finger on his chest. "You'll say it right—from your heart to hers. You'll say it right."

CHAPTER THIRTY-ONE

Maybe it was a good thing that the last day Martin spent on the beach with Myra was like so many other days they'd spent there. In the late morning Myra, feeling a little chilled, placed herself between Martin's two big bare feet as he sat on the Adirondack chair.

When the sun grew hotter, later in the day, Myra retreated to the shadow beneath the chair. A few hours later—the time went too fast for Martin!—the first signs of dusk came, and Martin lifted Myra onto the towel on his lap so that they faced each other.

The wind was starting to come up. A few large, dark clouds scuttled by and the soft tamarack trees on the rocky point made music in the breeze, and it was the saddest song Martin ever heard. As Myra faced him, she stretched and turned her long neck toward the lake, her usual sign that she was ready to head back to little Feaster Bay, the place she now called home.

Martin gently lifted her off his lap and placed her on the sand so she was still facing him.

She extended her neck and looked upward at him. Now there was no doubt that she seemed to know this was not going to be just like any other day. She knew it was late in the summer now, so it might be time to say good-bye—for the year, or at least she must have thought.

Martin hunched over so he would be closer to her. He noted again that sweet face looking up at him, the face that always seemed to have a little smile on it. He felt like he might be ready to cry, but he took a deep breath and stead-ied himself: "It's been a good day, Myra."

"We *always* have good days...you and me. Those are the best days of all, right?"

When he heard this, Martin considered for a second giving up the whole idea of taking the job and leaving Orenda Lake and Myra behind. But life, he knew now, had the force of a current always moving forward. He must do what he had to do.

"Myra, do you remember that first summer when it came to an end and you learned the word 'goodbye'?"

"I never liked goodbyes," Myra said very softly. She then shuffled her webbed, clawed feet and turned in the sand a little, and moved a few inches forward to get a bet-ter look at Martin's face.

"I always felt sad saying goodbye to you too at the end of the summer, Myra."

Myra paused and thought for a second. "But when it hurts,"—she was trying so hard to get the words right— "I know it will be all right... because... I'll see you next sum-mer."

Martin nodded and tried to speak, but he couldn't.

Myra went on: "I get happy thinking about the fun we'll have next summer. We'll swim together again...or just sit in the sun...and talk. We like to talk about things, little things and sometimes big things...but I kind of like the little things...so when you come back next...."

"But that's just it, Myra. This is a different sort of good-bye."

Myra stretched her long neck and searched his face: "But, but I'll see you next summer and then the summer after that, and then...."

Martin shook his head; "No, not next summer, Myra. I guess...I guess you'll have to get along without me. You're strong, Myra, and I'll always be thinking about you. You'll get along just fine, really."

"But I don't *want* to 'get along' without you. We're friends, right? The best of best of best of friends, right?"

"Myra, there's a place far away from here where I have to live now. It's a different place than here. You couldn't live there and be free. I want you to be a free and wild little creature, Myra. This is your home."

"But couldn't I swim to where you're going? Maybe I could find a river...and another...and I don't mind walking. I'm a little slow maybe." When she said "slow" she let out one of those quick little burping laughs.

"Yeah, you're a little slow," Martin said, laughing softly. He shook his head: "Myra, people have to move away sometimes, and it can be a lot farther than a turtle could swim or walk. Your home is right here on this lake. And you'll be okay. And who knows? Someday, maybe someday...." But he knew it wouldn't be right to promise anything now.

Myra was quiet for several minutes. Finally, she asked a question, "But will you stay here...just for now? Just to see me off?"

"I sure will, Myra. I sure will. I'll stay as long as you

want." He then lifted her up to the level of his eyes and looked again into that face with its sweet, upturned mouth. When he set her down again in the sand, he kept his hand on top of her shell and they both looked out at the lake.

After a moment or two, Myra began to move her feet: "It's dark, Martin. Bye, bye now. Until...." She didn't finish the sentence. She began moving toward the water. Martin knew enough about turtles to know that once they'd made up their mind about which way to go, they kept moving.

It was dusk by now and there was a big orange moon leaving a tint on the waters of Orenda Lake and all the trees around the lake looked like they were brushed lightly with a red-gold tint that was now fading away in the darkening dusk light.

As she trudged toward the water Martin called out to her, "You've meant so much to me, Myra. Never forget that, okay?"

Myra stopped just at the water's edge and turned her head back toward him: "You and me, right?"

"You and me forever, Myra."

Myra thought about this: "Forever? Is it that like 'always'?"

Martin could only nod. As Myra swam out onto the lake, Martin walked to the edge of the shore and watched her swim away. The early moonlight shone in the top of her shiny black shell. Soon she would be out of sight.

Martin felt lonely. Finally, he heard Cress's voice call down from the path. She must have seen Myra swimming away because she stepped out onto the beach and called out: "Goodbye, Myra. Goodbye, you little painted goddess! We will remember you."

CHAPTER THIRTY-TWO

At the end of the summer when Martin had said what was likely his final goodbye to Myra, he and Cress moved to San Francisco. He would now begin his new job as the executive director of the Pacific Center for the Study of Turtles. It was hard for Martin to leave behind his summer home at Three Tamaracks. It was also hard for Cress who had grown up near Glacier Pond and still had a sister and a brother who lived near there.

For a turtle lover, the Center where Martin worked had every kind of turtle he could imagine, but most were from North America. Each was in glass enclosures that re-created the turtle's natural habitats with carefully placed plants, flat and round rocks, water for swimming, logs, and whatever else made the turtles feel at home. Among the collection were Mississippi Mud Turtles, Loggerhead Musk Turtles (who sometimes gave off a strong odor) and Red-eared Pond Sliders; Box Turtles who insisted on their privacy, Eastern and Western Painted Turtles, Soft-shell Turtles and one Mud Turtle who seemed to avoid the mud.

There was a turtle species named a Stink Pot and another called a River Cooter. There was a Florida Red-Bellied Turtle, a Spotted Turtle, a genial and welcoming Wood Turtle, and many, many more. There was one irritable Snapping Turtle named Kong, but one day he got so mad he snapped and had to be returned to his swamp in the wilds. After being released, he was more than happy to plod away into a muddy bog and leave all people behind forever.

On the main floor of the center was an enormous aquarium set aside for sea turtles. Some large ones were brought in so they could recover from injuries. There were also small hatchling sea turtles that were brought in when a sudden cold snap hitting the shoreline might have killed them. Martin was very serious about the cause of protecting and conserving turtles, and he learned to keep in contact with the people who looked after sea turtle populations. He loved watching the big and small sea turtles use their flippers like wings as they swam their way in circles inside of the big aquarium. It brought back the memory of when he was a boy with a snorkel who swam with his friend Myra and watched her graceful motions when she was underwater.

Much of Martin's job meant being in an office on the third floor where he worked on budgets, made calls, and talked to his curators. Curators were the people who located, purchased, and arranged transportation for new turtles who were to be brought into the center. Though he was often in his office, Martin always found a way each day to go down to where the turtles were on display. He freely talked to all the turtles. When he hired young people as keepers who watched over the turtles and fed them, he made sure that they were animal lovers. He knew if they loved the turtles, they would take good care of them and would always enjoy their jobs.

It was a real delight when he learned that the young men and women keepers were coming up with names for all the resident turtles. Pretty soon each turtle had a name. There was Mable, Humphrey, Erasmus, Edith, Gordo, and Ursula, in addition to Durwood and Denise who were a breeding pair of desert tortoises. Other names were Tolstoy, Gertrude, Liz, and Ozzy. Isabelle and Frank were Western Chicken Turtles. There was also Yvette and Isosceles, a mated pair of River Cooters.

Like Martin, the young keepers always talked to the turtles they took care of and began to see as friends. Maybe even a few heard the turtles talk back, but they probably kept it to themselves. Few people are ready to admit to hearing turtles talk, but who is to say that type of magic does not happen to a few lucky animal-lovers?

Cress who had always been interested in photography took courses at a local university. After a while, she got into the field of wildlife photography and especially birds. Because she lived near the ocean, she began to photograph sea and shorebirds. Sometimes she traveled back to the northeast and returned with a treasure trove of photos that eventually served as illustrations in a handbook for birdwatchers called *Forest Songbirds of the Northeast*. Some of her framed photos were put on exhibit at a gallery in San Francisco and Martin was very proud of her.

Martin and Cress brought Nonie with them when they moved to the West Coast. The wall of Nonie's bedroom was filled with photos of Orenda Lake and Three Tamaracks. Some went back to when it was just she and the man she knew as Cyrus (but Martin called Papa Cider) were a loving childless couple for years at their camp. Other photos took on color with the arrival of the adopted boy named Martin who would become their son. The photos traced his growth from one summer to the next. One sun-blazed photo showed him reading in an Adirondack chair with the turtle he named Myra at his feet—she too was part of the family and appeared in several photos. On her night table next to the bed Nonie kept a large standing photo of her beloved Cyrus who seemed to smile and look directly at her as she opened her eyes each morning.

Martin became an authority on turtles and gained a certain amount of fame. He wrote eight books and also became an advocate for the conservation of both sea and land turtles. He spoke at universities and in front of conservation groups. His message was always to encourage people to love and appreciate turtles.

Martin knew he was living a blessed life. When he thought back to the days of his childhood when he lived in a boys' home he marveled at how far he had traveled in life. He had a loving life partner and had been brought up by two people who adopted him and changed his life. He also had experienced an actual talking friendship with a turtle and an otter and a snow goose. He had embarked on a journey up a river and discovered the secret of what had scarred his mind and body when he was just a very little boy. Also, how many have seen a Piebald Deer? What a life he had lived! What more could he ask for?

The decades passed and Martin's life entered a new phase. He reached the age of seventy and knew it was time for him to retire. The employees who worked with him over the years wished he could stay on. Still, he wanted to make room for a new person to be the head of the Pacific Center for the Study of Turtles. The time had come.

They had a grand reception at the Center to celebrate Martin and his contributions to the conservation of turtles and all he had done to make the Center world-famous. Even the turtles in their enclosures watched as Martin gave a speech in the display gallery to the employees, the many donors, and to friends Martin and Cress had met over the years. He felt great thankfulness for all that happened in the last forty or so years, and yet...and yet, there was still a sense of incompleteness he felt. What was he missing? What was he longing for? What was left in his life to be completed?

Many days he thought back to his friend Myra. She seemed a long way in the past now, but she, a simple Painted Turtle, had played such a large part in his life. It was because of her that he had decided to live a life dedicated to the care and protection of turtles. When he thought of her and the family camp and summer days on Orenda Lake, there were pangs of sadness and loss he always felt deep inside, but he didn't know what to do about it. He had never gone back and was afraid to do so. Myra had probably vanished by now, and what would be left of Three Tamaracks after all these years? What could he do about this sad sense of longing he still felt after so many years? Luckily for him, Cress knew exactly what he needed, and she set about to make it happen.

CHAPTER THIRTY-THREE

When Martin got out of the car, the smell was familiar. It was the scent of damp balsam needles that seemed always to have been in the air when he was at Three Tamaracks in the early years of his life.

Cress had bought him a plane ticket to New York because she knew he had to go back and see the family camp once more. She understood how he had avoided going back for all these years maybe because he was afraid all had changed at Three Tamaracks and it would not be the same place that he held in his memory.

He began to make his way slowly up the path to the cabin where he'd once spent his summers. He wasn't sure what he'd find because it had been over forty years since his last visit.

There had been several owners over the years, so he had no clear idea about what changes may have been made at Three Tamaracks over the years. Also, would Orenda Lake still be as wild and magical as it was in his boyhood?

As he neared the cabin, it looked much the same—the

same pine-bark on the outside, the same porch, and the stone chimney, but now with a few loose stones in the chimney. Papa Cider would not have appreciated that. Martin winced when he saw a satellite dish on the roof.

On the porch was a large man, probably in his late thirties. He was on a cell phone and when he spotted Martin, he gestured to him, distractedly waving him toward the porch. The man was in what sounded like a pretty tense conversation: "You tell him that if he doesn't get the financing by Tuesday, he can go rub rock...hello, hello...still there....?"

He looked up at Martin who was now a slender senior citizen with silver hair that was still thick. He wore glasses and was not quite as tall as in his younger years.

"This cell service up here is so bad." the man said. "They just put a tower up on Patchen Mountain, and you still can't get a signal. Can you imagine that in this day and age? By the way, I'm Tucker. I think we talked on the phone."

"I'm Martin. Nice to meet you."

"So, you owned this once, Martin?"

"My father, Cyrus—or Papa Cider, as I called him—built most of it."

"Not a bad place," Tucker said wiping off his sweating face with a handkerchief. "It's worth a fair bit of money now. I've thought of selling, but I'll probably bide my time."

There was some loud laughter from inside the cabin, followed by some yelling.

"You guys keep it down in there," Tucker said, "and lay off those games for a while! Take the boat out, will you? That's what I bought it for."

Martin looked out at the lake. "Well, Tucker, I have a lot of memories of this place, and I was wondering if you'd mind if I headed down to the beach."

"No, not at all. My daughter Amelia is out there sketching. She's an artist. Paints and draws all the time. I told her she'll never make a living that way, but what can you tell a twelve-year-old these days?" He shrugged and began looking at his mobile phone again.

Martin nodded and began following the pebble path down to the beach. He noticed the lake was louder than it used to be with lots of bigger and faster boats crisscrossing the water. As he reached the end of the path he saw Amelia. She was sitting in his old, newly painted Adirondack chair. She wore blue jeans and a light-blue smock over a t-shirt as she intently moved her drawing pen over a sketch pad. Martin noticed immediately that her hair was the same color as Nonie's and was fashioned into a long ponytail.

When Amelia saw Martin coming, she rose out of her chair and extended her hand: "Hi there. I'm Amelia. Are you Martin?"

"That's me. How did you know my name?"

"Oh, my dad said you were coming. Nice to meet you."

"And so nice to meet you, Amelia."

Standing up, she looked tall for her age. She was shy and abashed in a sweet-natured way, not quite sure what to say next.

"Could I look at what you're sketching, Amelia?"

"Sure," Amelia said, handing over her sketch pad. "I was trying to draw that duck over there who keeps swimming in big circles. Seems like he's lost. No other ducks around him. He's a mallard. I try to draw animals and trees and lake scenes and things, but I'm not very good yet."

Martin looked at the sketch, "Well, I disagree, Amelia. That sketch is nice. You're very good at this, aren't you? If I were you, I'd keep at it. You're talented. Anyone can see that."

She reached over to the sketch and pointed out details with her index finger that had purple fingernail polish on it: "Those big white pines in the background are *so* hard to do...and the mallard keeps moving and moving, but I watch the animals pretty closely. I'm doing the drawing in pen-and-ink, but later on, I'll splash on some tints of watercolor."

"Wonderful!" Martin said as he looked at the sketch.

He reached down for one of several sketch pads that sat in a pile near the chair where she was drawing.

"Would you mind if I...?"

"Not at all," Amelia said, "my family thinks I'm crazy to just sit out here and paint and sketch all the time. I'm glad *someone's* interested."

Martin turned the pages and studied each one. Amelia drew many animals—there was a woodpecker, a baby otter on a floating dock, a bullfrog, and several deer. Sometimes she did lake scenes like one of the mist rising in the morning from the water in the cove. As he continued to look through the sketches and watercolors he suddenly stopped: there was a watercolor painting of a Painted Turtle. After a few more pages there was another of the same turtle, and then another. He could barely speak and when he did his voice trembled a bit: "Amelia...these turtles...are they all the same one?"

"They *are*," Amelia said. "It's a turtle that comes up on

the beach here at least once a week. Looks like a female to me because they have shorter claws on their feet than the males. She has moss on her shell, so she must be really old."

Martin looked a little faint, "No, it couldn't be" he whispered to himself. "Not after all these years. She'd be so....old."

Martin lifted up one of the sketches of the turtle and noticed what looked like a familiar smile on the little face of the turtle.

"Martin, are you all right? Do want to sit down?"

"Oh, I'm fine, Amelia. So, you say she comes back to this beach a lot and looks very old?"

"Yeah, that's right. What do you think she's looking for, Martin?"

"Oh, maybe...maybe just a friend. Could you be a friend to her, Amelia?"

"Sure. I like her. She sits near my feet sometimes when I'm drawing. I wonder how she became so friendly. Sometimes when she looks up at me, I could swear she was smiling."

Martin took off his glasses and rubbed his face; then put the glasses back on again.

"It was so nice meeting you, Amelia. I'm going to send you a letter in a couple of weeks and tell you about that turtle. She's very special. So, watch for the mail boat. And in the meantime, you keep on sketching and painting, okay? I'm no expert, but I think you're going to be a fine artist. In fact, you already are. By the way, that turtle's name is Myra."

Amelia smiled and cocked her head as if she were a little puzzled. "Okay, well that's what I'll call her from now on—Myra. Yes, I *do* like that name! Goodbye now, Martin."

"Goodbye, Amelia."

Martin walked past the cabin where once he laughed with Papa Cider and Nonie. It was quiet now as he headed down the path toward his car. He looked out toward the beach where Amelia was back to her sketching. Then he said a few short words—to Cider and Nonie, to the lake, to the trees, to a young artist, to a chatty otter and flustered, lovely snow goose, and, most of all to a stalwart, full-hearted turtle who had become his best friend. He stopped and spread his arms as if to embrace them all as he said the words: "Thank you. Thank you very much."

EPILOGUE

As he finished his story, Martin smiled at the memories, but Rory was on the verge of tears: "But Uncle Marty, did you go back to Three Tamaracks after that?"

"Well, Amelia got my letter. For a couple of years, she sent letters and postcards telling me about Myra's comings and goings. I know she must have become a good friend to Myra. But little girls and little boys grow up and move on, and eventually the letters stopped."

Rory was still not satisfied: "So Myra must have been left *alone* up there."

Uncle Marty sighed and extended his hand to Rory: "Rory give me a little hand and help me out of this chair, if you will."

When he rose up, he swayed a little as he looked down at his great-grandnephew: "I'll just bet the rest of the family wonders why an old fella like me would buy a big house like this."

"Yeah," Rory said, "Mom and Dad worry that you'll fall down, and they wonder about how you can get up those big stairways."

"If you'll hand me that cane, Rory, I think we should take a little walk right now."

Walking unsteadily on a cane, Uncle Marty followed Rory out the back door of the house. They came to a small lawn in the backyard. It had tall pines in back and a trail that led into a small patch of woods.

"Let's just see what's back here, Rory. I wonder what's past these tall trees."

As they walked the narrow path they could see something very bright just past the trees. It was the afternoon sun reflecting on the water.

"I never knew *this* was back here," Rory exclaimed. "Wow, it's like a lake!"

The path now opened to a clearing and there was a pond in front of them; it was about an acre in size.

"Not quite a lake, Rory, but a good-sized pond. This pond is why I bought the house."

Rory looked out over the water: "Can you fish in here, Uncle Marty?"

"Oh, there are a few fish, but I leave them alone. But what I want you to do now is look out at that one big reddish rock jutting out of the water. Take a good look at it and tell me what you see."

Rory shaded his eyes and looked out at the rock, "Well I just see a big rock with a small dark rock on top of it...but, but...wait a minute..." Roy began to lose his breath.

"Yes, go on, Rory. Keep looking. "

"That dark little rock just moved...it's walking...it's a *turtle*...it's...it might be... MYRA!"

The very old turtle on the rock had moss on her shell. She extended her neck which had bright yellow stripes.

She moved a few inches out and found a perfect place in the sun. She stopped and extended her back legs outward so she could feel the warmth of the sun on her legs. She then stretched her long neck and turned her head toward the shore where Rory and Uncle Marty could both see what looked like a smile on her very small face.

Uncle Marty called out: "Good afternoon, Myra! I'm sorry I missed you this morning."

Myra slowly closed her eyes and began to doze on the warm, sunny rock.

"She must be really old now," Rory said solemnly.

"Oh, Rory, she probably is one of the oldest Painted Turtles in the world by now. But she's a happy old turtle. And what a heart! It's a heart so big, why it's fed by all the wild rivers in the world. Now let's head back and give her some rest. Remember we have my birthday party to go to."

As they began to walk away and up the path, Rory took Uncle Marty's hand: "But is it all true, Uncle Marty? I mean *really?* It's a good story, but after all, I didn't hear her talk."

At that very instant, the tiniest of voices called out over the pond water, and it could barely be heard amidst the wind and the bird songs that afternoon. It was now a tired little voice, but the words were cheerful and distinct: "Happy birthday, Martin!"

Uncle Marty turned around and called out: "Well, thank you, Myra. I'll see you bright and early tomorrow morning, okay?"

"She *does* talk!" Rory said, barely able to contain himself.

Martin just smiled when he heard this and he gently patted Rory on the top of his head.

"I did hear her. I know I did!" Rory said. "You know

what, Uncle Marty? I love that turtle, and I hardly even know her."

Uncle Marty rested his hand on Rory's shoulder as they walked. "Well, you're going to be all right, Rory. I just know it. This will be a summer you'll remember. I will too. And aren't I the lucky one? I get to spend another summer with Myra. And you will too."

ABOUT ATMOSPHERE PRESS

Atmosphere Press is an independent, full-service publisher for excellent books in all genres and for all audiences. Learn more about what we do at atmospherepress.com.

We encourage you to check out some of Atmosphere's latest releases, which are available at Amazon.com and via order from your local bookstore:

Saints and Martyrs: A Novel, by Aaron Roe

When I Am Ashes, a novel by Amber Rose

Melancholy Vision: A Revolution Series Novel, by L.C. Hamilton

The Recoleta Stories, by Bryon Esmond Butler

Voodoo Hideaway, a novel by Vance Cariaga

Hart Street and Main, a novel by Tabitha Sprunger

The Weed Lady, a novel by Shea R. Embry

A Book of Life, a novel by David Ellis

It Was Called a Home, a novel by Brian Nisun

Grace, a novel by Nancy Allen

Shifted, a novel by KristaLyn A. Vetovich

Because the Sky is a Thousand Soft Hurts, stories by Elizabeth Kirschner

ABOUT THE AUTHOR

From the time he was an infant Marc Douglass Smith has spent part of each summer in the Adirondack Mountains in northern New York. The Adirondacks are the setting for *Tamarack Summers* as well as many of his poems which have appeared in *The Fourth River, Snowy Egret, Green Fuse, Blueline* and other journals. He is a retired English professor who received his doctorate from State University at Buffalo. In retirement he continues to teach courses in nineteenth century American literature in the Osher program at Dartmouth College. He lives in New Hampshire with his wife Betsy, a watercolor artist.